KNIGHT ERRANT

A'ZEDI SURVEY CORPS
BOOK 1

BLAZE WARD

KNOTTED ROAD PRESS

Knight Errant
A'Zedi Survey Corps: 1
Blaze Ward
Copyright © 2025 Blaze Ward
All rights reserved
Published by Knotted Road Press
www.KnottedRoadPress.com

ISBN: 978-1-64470-459-2
Cover Art:
ID 285726170 | Spaceship © Philcold | Dreamstime.com

Cover and interior design copyright © 2025 Knotted Road Press

Reviews

It's true. Reviews help. Even a short one, such as, "Loved it!" So please consider reviewing this book (and all of the ones you've read) on your favorite retailer site.

Never miss a release!

If you'd like to be notified of new releases, sign up for my newsletter.

http://www.blazeward.com/newsletter/

Buy More!

Did you know that you can buy directly from the Knotted Road Press website?

https://www.knottedroadpress.com/shop/

CONTENTS

ALSO BY BLAZE WARD

The Science Officer Series

Start with: The Science Officer

The Jessica Keller Chronicles

Start with: Auberon

CS-405 (Command Centurion Kosnett, part of Jessica)

Start with: Queen Anne's Revenge

First Centurion Kosnett (sequel to Jessica)

Start with: Encounter at Vilahana

Additional Alexandria Station Stories

Alexandria Station Collection

Handsome Rob (Alexandria Station Universe)

Start with: Can't Shoot Straight Gang

=====================

Corsac Fox

Start with: Flight of the Corsac Fox

Operation Marrakesh

Start with: Trial by Leviathan

Captain Daring

Start with: Revoked

The Hunter Bureau

Start with: Mirrors

Fairchild

Start with: Fairchild

Last Stand

Start with: Lost Dreams

The Lazarus Alliance

Start with: Escape

Shadow of the Dominion

Start with: Longshot Hypothesis

Star Dragon

Start with: Birth of the Star Dragon

Kincaide's War

Start with: The Eden Package

Star Tribes

Start with: Winterstar

Blaze also writes Action-Adventure Here

For a whole cast of lunatics who wanted to be Tuckerized.
You might recognize a few of these people. Blame them.

PART 1
KALYN BLACKFORD

ONE

Maddox had expected to receive a note to report to that ominous building he'd visited with Captain Boru and Nyssa Taggart when he got back from his leave. Instead, he'd been directed to an innocuous parking lot, then picked up by a slick skycar and hauled outside of the city of Roydon to what looked like a big nature preserve in the middle of nowhere.

Until he saw the massive stone palace sitting in the middle of a cleared field probably fifty hectares in size. Including a hedge maze. Seriously.

They landed on a concrete platform in the front yard, where he was met by an older man in a civilian suit and absolutely no smile at all.

Maddox already felt out of place in his newly upgraded uniform, showing him as a Knight now and with a blank spot where he had removed *Marrakesh*'s unit patch. He felt a bit naked with that bare shoulder, at least in his mind.

"This way, Knight Nevin," the man said, gesturing Maddox to follow him, even as the skycar took off and headed back into town.

Maddox followed, up a slightly winding path of big paving stones that were a pretty rust color.

The building was gray marble. Three stories tall. Four hundred meters wide. Probably forty meters thick.

HUGE.

They slipped in a side door that felt like the servant's entrance, then went up a quick flight of steps, turned back, and up a second.

Top floor, not accounting for any attic concealed by the soft pitch of the roof.

Wide hallway as he followed the silent guide. Rough polished marble shot through with blues and blacks. Art on the walls that looked hand-painted. Things on pedestals that were probably art.

If you knew what you were talking about. Maddox kept his opinions to himself.

Eventually, he ended up in a...room. Sure, call it that.

Eighteen meters deep. Thirty or more wide. Four meter ceilings following the pitch of the roof.

Decorations...

Okay, maybe call it a library that got out of hand. Lots of books. Real ones. Printed on paper and bound. More art. Tables, desks, and sofas to read at. More arranged to talk to people. Patio visible out floor-to-ceiling windows interrupted by a single door not far from a fireplace.

Two people immediately visible by the fireplace, not counting his guide, who ushered him in, stepped back, and closed the door.

Thankfully, Maddox knew one of them on sight. And the other by image and reputation.

What he didn't know what was the hell he was doing in a room, on an apparent private estate, with Mariami Gelashvili, the Permanent First Secretary (Civil Service): *A'Zedi* Intelligence Operations. Nor with Fleet Marshal (F3) Thaddeus Drayton, Chief of Staff of the *A'Zedi Survey Corps* itself.

At least Gelashvili smiled when he entered.

"Maddox, good to see you," she said, rising.

Maddox nodded and approached. Drayton's eyes didn't seem to miss anything, like a gun turret tracking Maddox across the room as the man also rose.

Drayton was taller than Maddox, but not by much. Lithe and muscular like a dancer, perhaps. Bio said mid-fifties, but he looked at least a decade younger. And had a firm grip when they shook hands.

"Marshal," Maddox said solemnly.

"Knight Nevin," Drayton replied. "There's drinks over at the bar. Fix yourself something and join us."

Trap Number One: drinking not with *your* superior officer, but everyone's. Do not get drunk. Do not get the slightest bit tipsy.

Trap Number Two: do not avoid alcohol entirely, as he might also decide that you can't hold your liquor.

Maddox nodded and made his way over, selecting the fixings for an amaretto sour, heavy on the sour, with extra ice. Alcohol mostly flavor at this point, but nothing dangerous.

He returned and felt Drayton weighing his soul as he took the third point of a triangle, a chair he sat on the edge of, instead of falling back into. A side table between he and the First Minister held the glass for now.

She was drinking a red wine. The Marshal had coffee adulterated with something besides milk from the smell.

Maddox sat and waited, a polite smile pasted on his face as he waited for Trap Number Three to spring.

Or Four, if you assumed that this might be somebody's personal estate that he found himself visiting today.

The silence stretched long enough to grow uncomfortable. Maddox was willing to outwait either of them. However long that took.

"See, Thaddeus?" Gelashvili said after a time, never losing the smile off her face.

"I will grant your stipulations, Rami," Drayton replied.

Then he turned those gun turret eyes back on Maddox. Hazel, but a brighter form than Maddox had ever seen.

"What does *First In The Field* mean, Knight?" he asked simply.

"It means that Survey Corps isn't just the tip of the spear, but frequently the entirety of it, sir," Maddox replied evenly. "That you are so far away that nobody can get there to save you if you make a mistake. At the same time, you will go places that might not have ever been visited by an *A'Zedi* vessel. Or at least in perhaps decades. The Corps is there first. Fleet Operations, Transport Command, Construction Command, and even Intelligence don't arrive until later, so Survey is the standard by which strangers will judge all of *A'Zedi*."

He fell silent there, then thought about it and grabbed his glass to take a quick sip.

At least the First Minister was still smiling. Maddox felt like he was maybe scoring points in a game whose rules nobody had ever explained to him.

Save that the Marshal and he wore the same uniform.

"And your various battles as Gunner of *Marrakesh*?" Drayton pogoed off in some random direction, possibly wondering if Maddox could keep up.

"They generally came after us first, sir," Maddox nodded. "Albany. Varfelis Station. Domnall. Captain Boru would have happily slipped quietly away all three times, but the enemy would not allow it. Afterwards, we rescued any stranded sailors we could and got them to safety. Don't know how many eventually made it home, but at least they were safe."

"And your actions as Gunner?" the man pressed.

"If you have to fight, win," Maddox said. "Again, Captain Boru's explicit approach. Take the other guy down as ruthlessly as you have to. Use every trick in the book and then add an appendix of new tricks for future Gunners to learn. Then turn it off again when you're done."

"Thaddeus, you're being an ass," the First Minister interrupted, then turned that smile on Maddox.

He was happy that she really liked *Marrakesh* and Captain Boru, and was willing to extend that his way. Felt like he was going to need it.

"Marshal Drayton and I have been chatting," she continued in a friendly, conversational way. "He has a situation on his hands. One that *nobody* is willing to solve, because then they would have to admit that they screwed things up in the first place. When I suggested that you were interested in a lateral transfer as part of your promotion, Nevin, he inquired about Boru's adventures."

Maddox nodded, but didn't speak. She hadn't asked him anything. Nor invited a comment. And most of what *Marrakesh* had been up to for the last year fell under Intelligence work. The extremely Top Secret kind.

Marshal Drayton grimaced, then relented.

"I have a ship, Nevin," he said quietly. "Utterly fantastic crew. Their commanding officer was killed a little over a year ago, and they've already burned through two replacements in that time. Both quit, one of them suffering an emotional breakdown sufficient to render him unfit for service."

Maddox shared the grimace. Someone so broken mentally or emotionally that they had to retire? What had happened?

"At the same time, I cannot promote the deck officer to command, for reasons that are not necessary to cover now."

"Thaddeus," the First Minister said pointedly, drawing the two of them into a staring contest.

"I do not wish to pollute his first impressions, Rami," the Marshal finally relented.

She acquiesced with a nod. Drayton turned back to Maddox.

"They are a hard crew to manage," Drayton continued. "But extremely professional. Competent. Sharp. If you cannot manage the task, it will not be a black mark on your record, Nevin, because I was set to simply break the entire crew up and start over with an empty hull before your name came up."

"Sir," Maddox nodded. "What do you need from me?"

"You will take command of the *A'Zedi* Patrol Corvette *Kalyn Blackford*, Knight," Drayton ordered simply. "You will undertake a sailing patrol and determine why the best ship I have keeps chewing up commanding officers and spitting them out on the strand. You will fix the problem if you can, or you will report directly to me that it cannot be salvaged. At that point, I might simply keep you and shuffle everyone else off to other boats. I do not know that you will have many missions that require you to directly contact the First Minister here, but that remains an option, and they may assign you other duties as situations arise. Questions?"

"First In The Field, sir," Maddox said simply, then paused. "Are they that good?"

"They used to be, Nevin," he replied. "I don't want to lose them, but without Kumar Das I'm not sure if anything can be done. He captured lightning in a bottle."

"I'm familiar with the concept from *Marrakesh*, Marshal," Maddox nodded.

"That, *specifically*, is why we are having this conversation, Nevin," Drayton said. "Here, outside Headquarters, where the three of us could talk."

"I'll do my best, sir," Maddox said.

"That's the key," Drayton replied. "Now, we will retire and have a meal where we will not talk about *Doctor Kay*, Knight. Instead, I want to hear more about *Marrakesh*, because I am certain that the files I have been *allowed* to read left out a great deal of detail."

The man rose, turning a knowing scowl on the First Minister, who simply smiled enigmatically back.

Maddox figured that the job interview had gone well enough to pass the first several hurdles.

He had several more to go.

Then a crew that was causing the Chief of Staff himself troubles enough to be broken up, if Maddox couldn't solve them.

But he'd wanted an adventure.

TWO

Maddox followed the directions across an empty landing field, making sure to look all directions and listen as big trucks and lifts moved containers and people around in a noisy ballet.

The *Orders To Report* had been specific, but Maddox had skipped arriving early or contacting anyone related to the ship before now. The previous CO had suffered a complete breakdown, been medically retired, and probably would live in fear the rest of his life, starting at shadows from the reports Maddox had been allowed to read.

These days, he had a much better understanding of the term *Malicious Compliance*. A crew following orders to the letter. Showing no creativity or verve, save how it would get directly under the skin of a martinet like Knight Avguri Senoky and drive the man mad.

And Maddox had poked around, calling in a few favors because Senoky had been three years ahead of him in school, so they hadn't crossed paths to the best of his knowledge. Prick, plain and simple. Lots of people that respected the man. Maddox still hadn't found anyone who liked him.

But then, a man like Kumar Das would be a difficult commander to follow.

Maddox checked his comm. About five minutes ahead of his own schedule. Probably had people over there a bit nervous that he hadn't appeared yet, but he came around the ass end of the corvette and found the crew formed up in ranks.

Full complement, according to the stack of document. Himself. A Deck Officer. Twelve division officers. Eighty enlisted.

Doctor Kay—aka *A'Zedi* Patrol Corvette *Kalyn Blackford* —had been bumped up on the maintenance schedule when the last CO went down, so the crew had been off recertifying, training, and taking personal leave, only today really coming back together as a group.

Meanwhile, Repair Commander Anna Kader had been acting CO, with her own drydock crew handling everything. As Maddox got closer, he could see her and a couple of engineering officers standing on one side of the top of the ship, and Armiger Narayana Yadav, his new Deck Officer, standing with the other thirteen and the rest of the crew at the bottom of the ramp.

Maddox had given this a lot of thought. And filtered everything through how Captain Boru would have handled it, were he here. Probably no better role model Maddox could call on.

He walked up behind his new crew, then circled to the right and caught the ones on that end by surprise as he came into their peripheral vision. A low buzzing started. He ignored it.

Armiger Yadav stood facing the ship. Maddox walked up next to the man as he set his duffel bag down. Then he took three steps forward to split the gap, still on the shore at the base of the gangway, before turning back to face the new crew, ignoring Commander Kader for a moment because he was still ahead of schedule.

"I am Knight Maddox Nevin," he announced in a voice pitched to carry to the back row corners. "Your new commanding officer. Command tells me that you used to be the best ship in Survey Corps, but have fallen on some hard times lately. Hopefully, a month off ship has given everybody time to adjust and relax, and today finds you ready to get back to work and remind the rest of Survey Corps that they should be buying you the beer when they see that name on your cap. Or see that patch on your arm."

He paused, scanning the whole mob right to left and watching the impact of his words. Again, Captain Boru, though maybe a little more of Commander Messier, because she knew people.

"Because we're fresh from drydock, the orders are a quick, two-day sail to test that everything works, then we'll return and drop off the base folks before we head out on a longer run. Nothing crazy this time around, because we're still figuring each other out. If you have questions, I expect them to bounce them up your chain of command to your superior, or your Chief. Or your Division officers. Deck Officer knows you better than I do, so hopefully most of it gets resolved before it gets to me. Later, I'll know all of you and things will be easier, all the way around. What I'm asking for today is your professional pride. *A'Zedi* Patrol Corvette *Kalyn Blackford*, your beloved *Doctor Kay*, used to be the best. That's what I've been told. Let's make that happen."

He didn't bother waiting for a response. Instead, Maddox grabbed his duffel bag and stepped to the gangplank, climbing to the top though stopping short of the line that marked the ship itself.

"Knight Maddox Nevin, reporting for duty," he said formally, pulling his documents from his pocket and holding them out to her. "Commander Kader, I have orders to take command of this vessel."

It was all a ritual, but that grounded him better than anything else as the woman took them, made a show of reading the page, then nodding.

"Knight Nevin, I stand ready to turn over command," she replied in a lovely voice.

Attractive woman, but Construction Command and way senior. Unlikely he'd see her again, unless the ship needed another full refurb, so he kept his smile polite.

Maddox took that fateful step onto the upper hull of the corvette. Onto the ship itself.

His first command. Hopefully, not his last one.

He came to rest facing the woman.

"Commander Kader, I am assuming command," he said.

She nodded and stepped back into line with her two engineers.

Maddox turned to look down over the crew, still organized well enough for this, but not a formal inspection.

Captain Boru had taught him that crews capable of passing a formal inspection at any given moment usually weren't all that great at anything else. And vice versa.

And these people had been the best, until a year ago.

"Deck Officer," he called, locking eyes with Yadav. "Have the crew board, stow, and be to stations for a launch inside of one hour. I will be in the Map Room. Report to me there when the ship is ready to depart."

Rather than wait, or supervise and possibly even score things, Maddox crossed the open space. The ship was a long, rounded off square tube with the command sail stuck up like a tower in the middle. This space was actually a patio where receptions could be held and meat barbequed when the ship was on the ground, like now. Or even floating, which it did when you had to land on a planet that was mostly ocean.

Maddox entered his new command, turned into the spiral staircase, and descended.

THREE

Maddox appreciated the map room. The main table was a flat display that could be used for a variety of purposes, while the walls contained shelves with both paper maps as well as various gazeteers showing courses and distances, supposedly to every place ever considered important enough to visit.

A whole bunch of three-ring binders, in any case. Useful if you ever lost your nav computers in the field.

He'd closed the hatch, fixed himself some coffee, and settled to review the current patrol paths, both the short one as well as the longer route. Out of the way of the crew boarding and getting to their stations. Letting Yadav handle them.

He'd figured it would take about fifteen minutes to get everyone settled, so Maddox was a bit surprised when the hatch opened after only eight and Armiger Narayana Yadav stepped in, closing it behind him.

Older man. Forty-four years old, and still only an Armiger. What Maddox had been a month ago.

Or perhaps the fact that Yadav was still in uniform—and still an officer—was the bigger surprise.

The *Sovereign Collective Directorate of A'Zedi* was largely run by a Party, though done as something of a republic. Below the Directors themselves were the Secretaries and other important officials. The military in all of its bits and pieces was as entirely apolitical as it could be, run by the civilians. And the Party.

Narayana Yadav had been selected as the fall guy. No other way to put it. The son of a Director had been killed in an accident, and the fleet had needed someone to blame. His name had come up.

At the same time, the records that showed him blacklisted also showed how exceptional an officer Yadav was. Maddox figured that, without that one event, he'd been answering to Captain Yadav, instead of commanding Armiger Yadav today. The man had integrity, skill, **and** friends.

Grounded forever, until Kumar Das—his former subordinate—had somehow convinced or blackmailed enough people to let Das get the man transferred over as his Deck Officer when Das was promoted to command *Doctor Kay*. Second-In-Command, when he had previously been assigned to a quartermaster billet at a junkyard armory in the middle of nowhere.

And Command would never promote the man again. That was plain from the records. Dumb, but politics, and all of the military's job was to do what the civilians in charge told them.

"There's coffee," Maddox pointed to the robot in the corner.

"I'm fine, sir," Yadav replied, coming to attention so precise it almost looked painful.

"Sit," Maddox ordered. "Let's talk."

The man unfolded enough to conquer the other stool, eyes never leaving Maddox's.

Maddox was back at the estate, dealing with Marshal Drayton from the other side of the equation. He understood.

"Figured it would take longer," Maddox opened, waiting and inviting a comment with his face.

"Someone put the fear of the Gods into them, sir," Yadav replied evenly.

Maddox nodded.

"Hopefully, that will last long enough that they remember they are professional sailors and act like it," Maddox said. "I've been briefed pretty well on the entire situation, Armiger. Some important people want this crew to succeed, but don't know how to manage that. I was up for promotion and lateral transfer from Transport Command to Survey Corps. Some folks with a lot of stripes like my former Captain, and put me here."

Again, he waited, but Yadav was looking for Traps. Not that there were any, but Maddox knew the man would be gunshy for a while. Third CO in a year. Previous two broken as failures.

Kumar Das hung over everything like a malevolent ghost. Captain Boru would have liked the man, from what Maddox had read of him. And heard from others he'd located.

"Does the crew trust you, Yadav?" Maddox asked, watching the man blink in surprise.

"Yes, sir," he finally replied carefully.

"Good," Maddox nodded. "I'll rely on you to run the ship, like a good Deck Officer is supposed to. We're new to one another, and I have a lot of ideas, but not all of them will work out. Especially not with a crew inclined to push back. That's okay, because I intend to lead from the front, rather than the rear. That's my nature. Just operating like a normal ship is a win for now. Can they do that?"

Again, a long, pregnant pause as Yadav took his measure. Maddox didn't mind. He'd watched Captain Boru and his relationships with both Kaitlin Lynch and Chance Messier. Learned a lot about how the command team should work. And how the boss should encourage the crew to excellence by treating them like adults. And professionals.

Senoky had never wrapped his head around that part.

"They can, sir," Yadav finally replied, having chewed on several responses first.

Maddox nodded once again. Reaching into his duffel bag, he pulled out the sailing directions he had written. Not anything more than a series of points they were to visit, and the sequence.

"Launch when ready," he said, handing them to Yadav. "Two days from now, we return to drop off the engineering crew after we're sure everything works, then head out on this pass to inspect several buoys and sensor arrays. I plan to spend most of my time here, in the wardroom, or my cabin, rather than taking watches next door on the bridge. That will change once they get more settled, so let the bridge folks know. Questions?"

"Plenty, sir," Yadav said, rising. "None of them you can answer at present. I'll get us in motion."

"Thank you, Armiger," Maddox replied. "We need to make this work."

FOUR

Narayana Yadav hadn't stopped the previous two COs from being so badly discombobulated that they'd given up, with Senoky possibly literally going crazy by the end.

Nevin looked like a man hard enough to survive what this crew might pull. And mean enough to win.

Plus, the unspoken bits suggested that command had grown weary of the shenanigans and were on the verge of shipping everyone off to different ships, likely with the same black mark next to their name as he had.

The worst billets. The ugliest jobs. The ends of careers.

Narayana wouldn't wish that on anyone, having been there.

Still, they'd kept the crew together. Kept him as Deck Officer. Maybe even given then a new CO who could handle these people.

At least one smart enough to let his Deck Officer handle most things, like you were supposed to do.

If you weren't an asshole control freak like Avguri Senoky.

Narayana made his way to the bridge and caught the

nervous looks from folks over shoulders. Nobody knew what to make of Knight Nevin, and Narayana didn't really have a solid lead yet, either, other than the man seemed to be willing to sell him as much rope as might be needed to hang him.

And all the rest of them.

He found the intercom and keyed it.

"All hands, stand by for launch to orbit," he announced. "Check in by stations."

Narayana moved to his own seat and strapped himself in, watching various lights flicker once, even if they were green already.

Everybody had been warned by the new boss that they were about to commit a shakedown cruise, so they better be ready. Or Narayana would start his own punishment list.

That was also the province of the Deck Officer. You only faced the commanding officer when you really fucked up. Most of them probably still remembered that.

Narayana would hammer it home while he sorted out this new commander.

He counted down from one minute, just to make sure, but everything was still green, so Narayana turned to Stenny Kellogg and nodded to the young woman.

Young. Hell, she could be his daughter. Most of the crew were a whole generation younger. If he stayed at this for a few more years, most of the officers likely would, too.

Tomorrow's problem.

"Kellogg, seal us up," he said simply, watching her hands move.

Tall, skinny woman. Runner by vocation, always on the treadmill. Sharp as a razor.

Above, the hatches all growled as bolts set.

"Vessel secured," she called back. "Sir."

They'd get used to including that on the end quickly enough, so he didn't bark at her.

Instead, he cycled through stations.

"Engineering, what is your status?" he asked as he opened the line.

"Nominal aft," Armiger Forslund replied.

Narayana nodded and cut the line. They still had a dozen dockyard folks aboard, intended to be ready to fix anything that suddenly broke or came loose when the ship was put to harder use than bench tests.

Still, new CO. New day.

"Kellogg, bring the thrusters online and stabilize them for lift-off," he called, listening as the roar got deeper and louder.

Ship like this could lift purely on thrusters, but had enough of a curve to the outer edges for something of a glide. Better than a brick, anyway.

"Stable and holding, sir," Kellogg replied after it all settled.

Here goes nothing.

"Bring us up to forty percent slowly, Kellogg," Narayana ordered. "Forward drift and upright."

"Forty slowly and forward, aye," she nodded, long, delicate fingers dancing across her controls.

Outside, he could feel that little lurch as the landing struts flexed, then lost contact with the ground entirely. *Doctor Kay* was in free flight.

May whatever gods and saints out there take pity on them all.

Narayana settled back and listened as things began to run.

They were only just beginning.

FIVE

Maddox had largely spent the last two days out of the crew's way, taking meals with the officers and watching silently as folks did all their various shakedowns before he *Accepted* the ship back into service.

Everything by the book. At least on paper. Slow and careful. Emotions in check. Orders clear and having a bit of ambiguity to let these professional sailors solve certain problems their way.

Marrakesh had been lightning captured in a bottle. Captain Boru had told him that before Maddox left, mostly to remind him that any other ship wasn't going to be as good.

At least on Day One.

Yadav had handled all the tests, like a proper Deck Officer was supposed to, all the way down to a short flight in Ghost-space to test those systems. *Doctor Kay* was a Patrol Corvette. Tiny compared to *Marrakesh*. Faster, both on rotary thrusters and Ghostdrives.

As one would expect from a Survey Corps vessel.

They'd returned and dropped off the engineers, after a few last minute fixes that had been necessary. Nothing bad. One pipe that had burst when overcharged, but he could order that whole run stripped out and replaced, and bill someone else's budget for it, so he had.

Better he had gear that folks trusted than risk.

Yadav was at the command station, after Maddox had gestured him to stay put. Maddox had settled off to one side, standing where he could watch folks operate. Yadav was running things, but they were a warship in formal service again, and needed to act like it.

Weirdly, a patrol corvette in Survey service didn't have many officers on the bridge.

Sabeen Abbas, the ship's Astronomer, was generally aft near the VLS bay, where the *Vertical Launch System* deployed buoys, probes, or communications relays. Maybe one of the four missiles aboard, if the situation was dire enough to warrant it. Similarly, the Gunnery Officer was usually forward with the single Twin Particle Cannon turret.

Maddox was getting used to having only enlisted crew in here. Expert Sailor Kellogg, he had learned, was probably best pilot in the crew, while Specialist Horan managed communications forward to the gun teams.

And he'd watched how they tensed up when he entered the bridge. Nothing Maddox could do about that right now, because he'd rather they be a little afraid of him and his wrath than not.

He just didn't like what that said about things. But it was what it was.

For now, open space in front of them. Mostly open space. Survey Corps was still exploring that new corner of the galaxy that *Marrakesh* had opened, when they'd gone to Sabahattin and found an old *Riffrost* base of some sort.

And natives.

Eventually, Maddox had been quietly promised that he would lead some surveys in that direction, but for now he had to get this crew rehabilitated much closer to home.

Or not.

And since Maddox was here, he just went ahead and spoke. Kellogg had been watching him out of the corner of her eye anyway.

"Deck Officer, are we ready?" Maddox asked.

"We are, sir," Yadav replied crisply. "Kellogg, is your course laid in?"

"Aye aye, sir," she said.

"All hands, stand by for Ghost-space," Yadav said into the intercom.

Maddox nodded and watched, but wasn't that worried. Not yet, anyway.

"Kellogg, take us to Ghost-space," Yadav ordered. "Mark Two for now, then accelerating later when we stabilize."

"Mark Two, coming up," she replied.

The ship jumped up into a kind of alternate dimension. Close enough to the normal one, but a place where light-speed was handled differently. Where Ghostdrives could push the ship to Mark Two. Two light years per hour. Conservative and safe as you tested everything. Just like yesterday.

Maddox gave it a few minutes, watching Yadav bring them carefully up to Mark Four and holding it there.

"Deck Officer, how fast could *Doctor Kay* go, if we pushed?" Maddox asked.

Partly curiosity. Partly playing a role right now.

He still caught Yadav off guard.

"Nominally, Mark Six, sir," the man replied after a moment. "Fresh from the yard, Seven is probably within reach. I'm not sure what our top might be today."

Maddox nodded. Felt his serious face turn into a grin. Noted Horan's flinch when he looked up.

"Let's find out," he said to Narayana Yadav.

SIX

Narayana kept the scowl from reaching his face.

Young officer. First command. Supposedly experienced crew.

Shit like this was going to happen.

Best they handle it now, while still relatively close to base. Close enough to call for help, anyway.

"Engineering, stand by to push on the Ghostdrives," Narayana said into the intercom.

"Define push, bridge?" Forslund came back quickly. "How fast are you looking for here?"

Narayana turned to Nevin and asked with his eyes.

The Knight took a step closer.

"As fast as you can get under controlled circumstances, Armiger," the commander said simply. "Better we know now than find out later."

Narayana could only imagine the grumbling aft, but Forslund was smart enough to mute the line first.

He hoped.

"Give me two minutes to set my people up," the Engineer replied.

"Good enough," Nevin replied, then stepped right back into his corner.

Narayana watched Kellogg's shoulders twitch and square forward. At least she understood how silly things might be about to get.

He waited. Nodded. Smiled.

"Kellogg, begin acceleration," Narayana ordered.

He didn't set a top. That would be defined by the engines themselves.

At least until something broke.

"Mark Five," she replied quickly. "Coming up on Mark Six."

"Engineering, how are your systems holding?" Narayana asked.

"Stable for now," Forslund replied.

Narayana nodded. Then leaned back and watched, understanding that Nevin had laid something of a trap for the crew.

And, truth be told, he also wanted to see how Kellogg would handle it.

She glanced back, but he didn't say anything, so she returned to her boards.

"Approaching Mark Seven," she called out in a voice starting to show some nerves.

After all, all Narayana had ordered was acceleration.

Outside, things were moving faster. Stars slid by on his screen fast enough to detect motion, instead of the jump you got with slower speeds and inattention.

"Seven Point Five," she said breathlessly after a bit. "Coming up on Mark Eight."

According to the original design, Eight should be the top.

Ludicrously fast, by any measure, though any number of smaller ships could blow past that number. Last he remembered, the record was somewhere around Twelve and a half light-years per hour. Experimental craft, stripped down as far as possible.

But science never slept, and every generation of warship tended to be a little faster than its predecessor.

"Crossing Mark Eight," Kellogg said, voice full of awe and wonder. "Point One. Point Two. Point Three. We seem to be leveling off, sirs. Eight Point Three-Five and more or less holding."

"Forward scan?" Nevin asked. "What's my navigation cone look like?"

Narayana found it interesting that Kellogg blinked and looked over at the man before returning to her own boards. Like disbelief had overtaken her for a long moment.

"Clear beyond four known stars ahead, sir," she said.

Nevin nodded.

"Adjust your course as necessary to remain clear of all of them," Nevin said.

Again, Kellogg's shoulders twitched.

Senoky would have issued a specific maneuvering course for her to adhere to. Nevin was letting her determine what it should be, without any greater direction.

She caught on after a moment.

"Aye, sir," was all she said.

Narayana nodded when Nevin glanced over. Message delivered. Nevin was trying to communicate to this crew that he believed in them.

Would they listen?

SEVEN

Maddox was in the Map Room. Actually working, instead of just staying out of Yadav's way. Kellogg and Horan had survived their trials and seemed a little more relaxed. *Doctor Kay* seemed none the worse for running at max speed for almost an hour.

Two days of cruising after that to get equipment and personnel a little more settled. A week aboard, getting everyone used to things.

As used to it as they might get. Someone had definitely put the fear of God into folks. Maddox presumed Yadav. Message delivered. Hopefully it would stick for long enough.

The hatch opened.

Maddox looked up as his Radio Officer stepped in. Junior to the Diplomat in the Diplomacy Division. Like everywhere else, a department made up of a senior officer, usually an Armiger, and a junior, usually a freshly-minted Squire.

Waters had a seriousness to him that went beyond normal duty. Kind of what you wanted in communications, where the ship was either talking to home from too far away, or talking to strangers and trying to convince them that you were friendly.

Assuming you were. Some of the folks out beyond national boundaries were there because they didn't want to belong to anything more organized than a single world or system.

"Sir, updated orders from home," Waters said simply, holding a printout in one hand and offering it.

"Executive summary?" Maddox asked.

Radio had to receive it, decode it, and understand it. Nyssa Taggart had always handled that for Captain Boru. Or one of her people.

"Distress signal received, sir." Waters got even more serious. "Garbled and cut short, so they'd not entirely sure what happened. We happened to be closest when the relay picked it up, but there are no ships known to be anywhere close to it or us. Proceed to coordinates and investigate."

"No mention of the nature of the disaster?" Maddox confirmed, already standing and gesturing the man back onto the bridge proper.

"Negative, sir."

"Let Corps know that we've moving to investigate," Maddox said, watching the man nod and turn away to his own station, in a cubbyhole at the forward end of the narrow bridge.

Maddox was still getting used to a bridge with no officers sometimes, but he had Senior Experts in all six divisions, and they frequently sat watch. Surveyor Chloe Gammon was in the command seat when he emerged.

She looked up a touch hesitant, but they were still feeling their way into a relationship. Tiny woman. Big personality. She started to rise and he motioned her back down, then handed her the note.

Kellogg was driving today.

"Pilot, stand by to come about and transition to Ghost-space," Maddox announced in a loud voice. "Let Engineering know."

He turned back to Gammon as she read the report and looked up at him with big, hazel-brown eyes.

"Sir?" she asked carefully.

"You have the deck," he reminded her, then stepped back.

She nodded and started typing on her console.

"Kellogg, destination has been transmitted to your station," Gammon said. "Lay it in and get us moving."

Maddox smiled and stepped back. Then slipped into the Map Room and located the binder he wanted, pulling it and returning to the bridge.

Couple of empty workstations at present, because the ship was under normal sailing, so he plopped his butt down and started reading.

He felt the ship lurch up to Ghost-space, and Yadav appeared a few moments later, eyes a little wild until he took in the tableaux. Yadav paused to button up his jacket before walking over to Gammon.

She replied by handing him the note silently. Yadav ended up in the next station over as Maddox worked.

After a few minutes, Maddox looked up, then slid the binder over for the man to read.

More time passed, the ship now barreling madly along at Mark Six, because he hadn't said anything to Gammon other-wise, letting her handle things until they needed to up the alert level or her watch shift ended.

"Middle of bloody nowhere," Yadav murmured under his breath. "What the hell were they doing out there?"

"Thinking they might have been taking a shortcut across to

this area," Maddox leaned in and pointed at a spot on the map. "That, or they were trying to get lost and found it."

A'Zedi sat in the middle, with the *Holy Imperium of Copez* anti-spinward and the *United Technocracy of Wronlori* spinward. The *Enlightened Tyranny of Traisa* was more or less rimward from *A'Zedi*, and a whole bunch of *Unaffiliated* systems were coreward.

And the starship *Livingston* somewhere in there, possibly lost or about to be.

"Gammon, estimated flight time from here?" Maddox asked, looking over his shoulder.

"Kellogg?" Gammon asked.

"Two and a half hours," Kellogg replied.

Maddox nodded, then checked the clock on the wall before he looked back at Gammon.

"One hour out, initiate a watch shift so everyone on duty is fresh when we get there," he ordered. "Don't come to alert until we get closer, but let folks know that we might be in an emergency when we do, and to mentally and physically prepare themselves accordingly."

She blinked at him. Pure surprise. Then her brain caught up and she nodded.

Maddox tapped Yadav on the arm.

"Let's talk in the Map Room," he said, rising.

EIGHT

Narayana followed Nevin into the other chamber, pausing to fix himself some coffee as the man settled at the big table. Senoky would have welded himself to the command station and remained there until the situation was resolved.

But Narayana had also come to a better understanding of what Nevin was about. The man was letting these sailors act like professionals. Treated them like adults who knew what they were supposed to do. As opposed to that micromanaging martinet that Narayana had watched break under the weight of the sorts of malicious compliance that this crew could manage.

Maybe there was hope?

"What are your orders, sir?" Narayana asked as they settled.

"I need to brief you, Mister," Nevin replied evenly, eyes about as deadly serious as they might get. "Close the hatch and sit."

Narayana did, wondering if the other shoe was about to drop.

"*Marrakesh* did things for people that we don't talk about with most of the Fleet," Nevin said in a dark, sober voice. "You will not repeat this conversation, or the folks that dislike you might have enough ammunition to finish the original job. Am I clear?"

Narayana blinked at the implications, then nodded. Expectant.

"We occasionally operated as a spy ship, Armiger," Nevin nodded. "On a recent mission, we had to track down a vessel that had strayed too close to a *Wronlori* base and gotten themselves into trouble. Sudden lack of communications to base, with no follow-up. In that case, we were hauling a Forward Repair Depot, and had to slip in quietly, starting repairs while waiting for the bad guys to notice us and come in firing. We got away afterwards, because Captain Boru is and was a fantastic officer and taught me a lot of good things."

He paused there and Narayana nodded.

Spy ship? And they put the former Gunnery Officer on a Survey vessel? What the hell did the Powers That Be have in mind for *Doctor Kay*?

Or was Maddox Nevin that good? That was always a possibility.

"I don't expect that *Livingston* got jumped by pirates or anyone else, but we're going to slide in as quietly as possible and look around, rather than just arriving and announcing ourselves to anyone that might be listening. *Doctor Kay* might be a Patrol Corvette, but we sure aren't armed to fight anybody serious."

Narayana nodded. At least Nevin understood that much, and wouldn't be a cowboy.

Probably.

"What do you expect?" Narayana asked.

"No clue, Deck Officer," Nevin suddenly smiled. "Could be a short-circuit knocked their radio off-line and they don't know how to fix it. Could be pirates. And there is a wide range of alternatives in the middle. We were closest, so command sent us. Might be other ships getting vectored down, but I doubt it. Probably waiting for us to call for help, but that means nobody can show up for a day or two and our asses are hanging out in the wind."

"Which is why you told Gammon to have everyone prepared for anything," Narayana nodded.

It made sense. And was just about as far from Senoky as you could get. Almost back to what life had been like under Kumar, but he was careful not to make that comparison.

Kumar Das had been one of a kind, as officers went. Smart. Sharp. Calm. Action-oriented.

It had caught up with him eventually, but not until after he'd rescued Narayana from the deadest of dead ends. Couldn't give him his career back, but at least he was still on a ship. And one where the new commander was trying to rescue him, it seemed.

Nevin had been watching Narayana think. He nodded to the man.

"How should we handle arrival?" Narayana asked.

"I want you in command, relieving Gammon," Nevin ordered. "Keep her handy, but she'll be at the end of five hours on duty, and starting to get a little punchy. We need to be ready to fight, to run, to scramble everyone in suits to rescue a dead ship, or to start scanning because the ship has disappeared and we'll need to find it."

He paused, eyes searching Narayana's face for something.

"I'd hoped for more time to gel with the crew," Nevin continued. "For them to get used to me. We're out of time, so I need them to reach back and remember who they used to be, before the dipshit I'm replacing came along. And the one before him. We are Survey Corps. *First In The Field*. That means first in the line of fire here, if it comes to that. Are they ready?"

"They should be," Narayana nodded.

"Good," Nevin nodded back. "Because it's our asses on the line."

Narayana kept the shiver inside, but agreed.

At least they were back in the adventure business.

NINE

Maddox had moved to the side of the bridge, letting Yadav handle things. Crew was prepped. Hyped, even, and ready to roll.

"Status?" Maddox asked the room, because he hadn't powered on a station to watch.

"Coming up on the edge of scanner range, sir," Waters called from the radio room.

Waters had stayed on duty, but also rousted the rest of his team, as well as all of the Survey department, who were actively working right now, most of them aft.

All hands on deck, as it were.

Maddox nodded, then fell silent and watched the crew work. Kellogg had taken a lunch break, then returned to duty, bumping Specialist Dituri by virtue of rank, seniority, and attitude. Exactly why Maddox preferred the young woman be flying them right now.

"Radio, any positive signals in your sphere as we close?" Yadav asked.

By the numbers. Exactly as the book said to do it, when

closing on an unknown and possibly hostile situation. Armiger Petra Veillon was forward with her guns. Horan was handling things from here. Hell, even the small team of combat troopers had suited up and were prepared for rescue or storming operations, as needed.

"Negative on signals, sir," Waters replied. "Scanning out to about four light-years right now and not picking up anybody transmitting."

Didn't mean they weren't there. Meant they weren't talking if they were.

"Slide us in quietly, Kellogg," Yadav called.

Maddox approved. Maybe an emergency like this was exactly what the crew had needed, in order to show off to the new CO that they weren't a bunch of fuck-ups. Like the previous CO had considered them, right up to the moment they broke him.

From his vantage, Maddox watched Kellogg steer them down onto the coordinates listed, slowing in Ghost-space until they were just puttering along.

"We're almost there," she announced to the room.

"Drop us at five light-seconds and prepare for anything," Yadav responded.

Anything, indeed.

They emerged in realspace. Middle of nowhere. Five light-seconds was an enormous distance if you wanted to fight. Just fine for scanning.

And outside of the sphere of danger, if someone was lurking to ambush you.

Hopefully.

"Survey Team, you are on," Yadav announced into the intercom.

"Stand by, Bridge," Astronomer Abbas replied from his

duty station aft. "I presume you still don't want to deploy a probe?"

"Not until you give me a good reason," Yadav said, looking over at Maddox for confirmation.

Maddox nodded in agreement. Yadav needed the crew to trust both of them. Best way to do that was to let them think and act. Without the micromanaging and passive aggressions.

"Scanner ping headed downrange now," Abbas said.

Maddox heard the system beep once quietly. Standard protocol, though Taggart had always either turned it all the way down, or all the way up, depending on the situation at hand.

"Bridge, I've got wreckage not far from coordinates," Abbas continued. "Not showing much power, but there's a hull in one piece."

They were too far away to resolve it more than a gray spot, but at least it was there.

"Anything else visible?" Yadav asked, like a proper Deck Officer.

"Nothing reflected on the light-speed wavefront," Abbas offered.

Yadav looked directly at Maddox now. Practically demanding orders, which was fair. He was only Second-In-Command, and Maddox hadn't been disabled in any way.

"Survey, split your operations in two," Maddox ordered. "Half the team focused on the new target. Other half watching the perimeter so nobody sneaks up on us as we approach."

"Understood, Bridge," Abbas replied. "Stand by."

Again, the wait, but someone had a powerful optical tele-scope pointed at the target now. Gyro-stabilized and locked in to the point that Maddox could see a bit of a slow tumble to the ship over Kellogg's shoulder.

"Anything anywhere?" Maddox asked the room. And the ship.

"Negative at present," Abbas replied.

"Kellogg, take us in," Maddox ordered, then looked at Narayana Yadav and ceded authority back to the man.

Kellogg simply nodded without looking back, so she was getting used to things.

They bounced up into Ghost-space for hardly long enough to matter, then dropped back down.

"Moving in on rotary thrusters," she announced. "Closing. Target has a slight spin at present. Also some roll and yaw. Whoa!"

Maddox flinched, then took a long step that put him right over her left shoulder to see what had drawn that reaction.

Battle damage. Somebody had hammered the ship aft with a particle cannon. Civilian ships didn't have a layer of armor like the military did it. Or the honeycomb of empty spaces or less important cabins that could absorb battle damage.

He was looking at *Northwind* again.

"Perimeter team, stay alert," Maddox ordered, stepping into command if they were facing combat. "Gunnery, are you watching this?"

"Affirmative, bridge," Veillon replied. "One shot, reasonably short range, limited deflection."

"Agreed," Maddox said. "Stand ready."

He turned to Yadav.

"Give me shipwide," Maddox said. "That way, everyone is listening and prepared."

The man took a moment, then flipped a switch and nodded.

"Flight Deck, this in the bridge," Maddox said. "Warm up *Packrat* and prepare for flight. Perry, your team will board and secure the vessel. Boyce, you will dock and see if you can kill the spin. Not sure that *Packrat*'s powerful enough, but at least you can get it stable enough for us to dock and finish the job."

"Roger that," Boyce replied.

He missed Walt Rafferty, back on *Marrakesh*, but Lead Expert Boyce always had a smile on her face. And was pretty good at small boat operations.

"Bridge, this is Perry," the marine called. "How many people do you want deployed?"

"As many as you can transport in one go, Perry," Maddox replied.

"Roger that," Perry said.

He had to make sure not to call the Squire *Pretty*. Maddox hadn't gotten the whole story, other than some sort of official typo at some point in the man's career that got past all the computers and onto official paperwork before it was finally corrected, so a lot of people teased him.

At their own risk, though, because Perry was tall at one hundred and ninety centimeters, though lean at about ninety kilos. Long, deadly dancer who knew just about every weapon, melee or beam, in existence. Just exactly who Maddox wanted on point right now.

Marrakesh had only had Cam Farrell, but Survey Corps frequently was working on hostile planets. As a result they had an entire exploration team of ground-environment experts on hand, ready for anything a CO might order.

Maddox wondered how hostile this one might be.

TEN

"Bridge, this is Perry," Steve said as he checked his gear one more time. "Ready for departure here."

"Flight deck is clear," Armiger Yadav replied. "Boyce will launch shortly. You clear the airlock and rendezvous with her outside."

"Roger that," Steve replied, checking everyone around him.

Packrat was a small shuttle. Basically two seats up front and two more where you could cram in people smaller than him, plus a cargo box that could be enclosed to haul things or left open in situations like this.

He'd had Boyce go ahead and open the thing up so he could put himself and three others aboard. Broom, Dowe, and Zavaleta. Good mix of skills, experience, and all smart.

"Seal it up," Steve ordered, waiting for everyone's status lights to go green on the outside before he pushed the button to close the airlock and start a cycle.

All of them were armed for bear, as the saying went. Ready for trouble.

Once outside, he saw Boyce had backed *Packrat* up and

they could drift over with a quick hop, magnets on hull to magnets on bed.

"We're aboard," he said once everyone had a hand gripping a stanchion.

"In motion," she replied.

Packrat gave a little lurch, then began closing on microthrusters. They'd started within about fifty meters of the derelict, then parked the big ship, so the jaunt across went quickly.

Slow tumble. All three axes. Damage aft from heavy weapons. No radio signals of any kind, including the usual emergency beacon folks tripped if shit got bad enough.

Whatever had hit them had moved fast, cut surgically, and then shut everything down hard.

He and his people were all armed with Disruptor Bombardiers, the carbine version of the heavier Light Disruptor Cannon that Dowe was rated on and not carrying today. Plus, Steve had his Vibropike, currently collapsed on his left hip opposite the Variable Disruptor on his right.

"Pretty, where do you want to dock?" Boyce asked as they got closer.

As Squire to her Lead Expert, he was in charge here. And senior ground trooper, too.

And she called him *Pretty*, but so did a lot of the enlisted folks. Generally a term of respect. Occasionally honest affection, but they were all sailors together.

"Close to the damage," he decided. "See if you can get a solid grip and kill the spin before we board."

"Coming up," she replied.

"Look alive," he said, switching to the team channel. "Eyes on all corners in case they left us a surprise or an explosive. Zavaleta, you've got point."

"Roger that," Porter said. "On point."

Expert Sailor Porter Zavaleta. Rated for Demolitions and Explosives Ordinance, because Survey Corps occasionally needed to do civil engineering on the ground.

Best to have experts on hand, just like Vanya Dowe was trained in powered boarding armor though they didn't currently have any aboard, and Serge Broom had the widest range of hostile climate training expertise on the crew.

Packrat nosed up against the freighter's hull. Medium-sized hull, right about the same dimensions as *Blackford*, but only a small crew compartment forward and a multi-bay cargo area in the middle, plus a small engine room aft and high, so you could drive trucks in while on the ground.

"Stand by for lock," Boyce announced. "Think we're good enough."

"We'll stay aboard," Steve replied. "Go ahead."

Last thing he wanted was to be inside if the ship was spinning. Right now, he and his people were safe, and would ride *Packrat* if it came loose.

"Bridge, this is Boyce. Stand by for maneuvering."

"Watching you from here," the Deck Officer replied, so it sounded like Knight Maddox had stepped back again.

Steve was still trying to figure out the new CO. Hard man, but not a hardass about it. Expert and sharp, but stood back a lot and let the crew work. Like here.

Hell, that punk Senoky would have been issuing orders about every single thing right now, so Steve already counted this as a win.

Steve felt the rumble in his boots as Boyce started pushing. Pulling. Something. The freighter was a solid wall in front of him, so he wasn't sure it was working and didn't want to turn and look back at *Blackford* to be certain.

"Bridge, what is your read?" Boyce asked after she shut things down again.

"Close enough to rest for now," Armiger Yadav replied. "Perry, you're on."

Steve nodded.

Time to go look inside and see what happened.

ELEVEN

Steve used backpack thrusters get himself up where he could look into the hole someone had blasted in the hull. Looked like engines, rather than cargo bay, so they were intending to kill the ship's ability to escape. And call for help, because the briefing notes Deck Officer had shared hadn't said anything about a second distress signal after the first.

Gash. About what he'd do with a sharp blade and a number one cut, right shoulder to left hip. Big enough that he could penetrate the derelict here rather than via any of the airlocks that someone might have boobytrapped.

"Zavaleta, check for surprises here," he ordered, back and up enough to be out of any shots from inside.

Scans hadn't shown any significant power, so someone had gotten the emergency batteries as well. Never a good sign.

Three of them took overwatch as Porter drifted close, not touching anything while shining a simple handflash around the edges and into the gap. Then a portable handscanner that any competent demolitions expert slept with under their pillow.

"No picking up any trouble," Porter replied. "Inside is

open to vacuum and looked like all debris call sucked out before we got here.”

Steve grimaced, but the only people who would see it were back on the bridge.

“Make entry, Porter,” he said simply.

Only one way to make sure there weren’t any bombs.

Porter grabbed the edge of the rupture and poked his head deeper inside, shining his light around from the motions of his arm.

“Engineering machine shop with bench tools,” Porter announced. “Secondary penetration through in interior bulkhead, but I don’t remember an exit wound.”

“Confirmed, Zavaleta,” Deck Officer replied. “Only the one battle damage visible.”

Steve nodded. Short range. Killing blow. Save the cargo to loot. Maybe kill half the crew in one shot.

Civilians. No luck against pirates.

Porter went the rest of the way in.

“All clear inside visible space,” he said. “I’m magnets on deck here. No light. No power. No anything.”

“Following,” Steve said simply, riding his jets down and in.

Empty room. Bench tools, as Porter had said. Nothing else, but that bolt would have cooked anything it could, then the air would have pulled it out. And the shot went through an inside bulkhead. Quite a ways.

“Bridge, confirming status,” Steve said. “We’ll move forward and locate the bridge. Channel will remain open, but I’m not sure how good our signal will be.”

“Understood, Perry,” the new CO was suddenly on the line. “Exercise caution until you have a better idea what happened.”

He nodded. Smiled even, then remembered they could see his face on one of their screens, so he got serious again.

Old punk would have had an annotated list of orders about now, half of them at odds with the other half and both utterly foolish.

New guy must have remembered that they all went to the same academy. And wore the same uniform.

"Zavaleta, find me a hatch forward," Steve ordered. "Look for places with atmosphere that might still have survivors."

"Moving forward," Porter replied.

"Broom, you have rear guard," Steve continued.

Quickly, they slid into something of a marching order for the corridors. Ship looked like it had two corridors forward. Or something.

"I have local power to the hatch," Porter announced after a quick inspection. "Both sides open to vacuum on the control panel readings. Opening now."

It moved. Died about halfway, but Steve was willing to bet that the heat in here had warped the frame. He'd seen it happen. Enough space to get through.

"Making entry into aft cargo bay," Porter continued his commentary. "Space appears empty. Repeat, empty. Dark. No cargo, locked down or floating."

Steve followed him into an auditorium with ten meter ceilings, walking on his magnets with a clunk clunk across the steel deck.

Someone had emptied the place. Had it started that way, or had someone moved with that much ruthless efficiency? If they'd panicked, he would have expected to find stuff left behind.

Nothing.

"Bridge, how many bays are we expecting?" Steve asked.

"Three from the design and scans, Perry," Deck Officer replied. "Confirm that aft is empty at present."

"Nothing," Steve said. "Moving forward to middle now."

Along the outer edges of the bulkhead there were hatches, with garage doors in the middle to let trucks move stuff around. Porter did his magic and they were into the next one.

Steve felt better. This space was about half full. And filled with some crap floating around. Helluva mess to see anything, but the ship hadn't been completely stripped.

They weren't facing off with impossibly good pirates. Or folks who had brought so many sailors and forklifts that they could strip the place like locusts in the few hours they must have had between the distress signal going out and the *Blackford* showing up.

"Bridge, you seeing this?" he asked, knowing that the camera on his helmet would be the one they watched.

"Affirmative, Perry," Deck Officer replied. "Make your way forward and worry about an inventory sheet later."

Porter was already in motion. Not a lot floating about. Just enough crap to be sure that something had gone wrong in here.

Forward bay was filled with cargo. Boxes strapped down properly. Everything in place. Cargo nets strung.

What he would have expected to find, without pirates.

"Bridge, this is Perry," he said, standing in the middle of the bay looking around. "I'm reading this as they ran while they were in the middle of stripping the hulk. Any chance we picked them up as we closed and know where to head to next?"

"Got the Astronomer looking now, Perry," Deck Officer replied. "You finish your run and I hope to have updates for you when you're done."

Steve nodded and gestured Porter into motion.

Maybe he'd get a crack at those pirates, after all?

TWELVE

Maddox had put Waters in charge on the bridge for now, drawing Yadav with him into the map room and summoning Astronomer Abbas forward.

His name always suggested darker toned than Maddox, but Abbas had turned out to be much a lighter ethnotype, though not the pale blonds more common in *Wronlori*. But the galaxy was a big place, and folks had moved around over however long to end up everywhere. And *A'Zedi* had the whole range of human coloration.

They were all three seated on stools around the map table, coffee mugs in hand.

"Perry's thought that they saw us and ran," Maddox said. "Any chance we might have seen them and not realized it?"

From the way Yadav and Abbas glanced at each other, Maddox assumed that Senoky would have been screaming at some sort of intelligence or intellect failure on their parts. Instead of asking an honest question.

"Nothing immediately obvious, sir," Abbas replied.

Doctor Sabeen Abbas, MS, PhD. Man had gotten his commissioning degree, then gone back for a doctorate in astronautics. Maddox presumed that Survey gave him the best chance to go out and see things, instead of writing grants from a cubicle on some campus somewhere. Kind like what Maddox had learned from the folks on the Sabahattin mission.

"Assuming that nobody's left here to jump us," Maddox nodded, "and we're not picking up any beacons from escape pods or sailors in suits, can you have your folks review those records? We can log this whole thing, but I'd like to find whoever did this. If they took prisoners, maybe rescue those folks. Or avenge 'em."

Both men nodded.

"What do our orders cover?" Yadav asked.

"Rendezvous with this ship, answering the distress call," Maddox replied. "Past that, blank slate, because there's nobody close enough to us at present. If we did call for assistance, that's probably a day away, unless they burned out their engines getting here, so we're on our own. You need to tell me if we have enough to pursue, or when we've hit a dead end and have to return to base. Or wherever we're headed next. Also, if they are lurking around here, maybe having gotten a little ways away and shut down to hide, make sure that the crew is ready to suddenly run or fight if they pop back up, trying to pounce on us or get away. Not like a Patrol Corvette is particularly dangerous, if we've got a pirate with enough firepower to kill a freighter like that."

"Sir?" Abbas asked, apparently confused.

"Single shot, close range," Maddox reminded him. "They they got in and killed all power except probably local emergency batteries. Then shut those down as well, before they opened the aft bay and started emptying cargo onto their ship. At some point, they were in the middle of the second bay and stopped. Perry is likely to find the ship emptied of crew and passengers, but maybe with some things forward that weren't stripped. If the pirate saw us and ran, did they run far? Or are they only a few light-minutes or light-hours away right now, shut down and hiding in the darkness until we move on? Not like we'd see them if they didn't make any noise. And if they are armed, they might come after us, so I want the crew to stay at an alert status for now. Not action stations at all time, but thirty seconds from it if we have to."

Yadav nodded crisply at that. Abbas needed convincing.

"Let me tell you about one of my first missions on *Marrakesh*, Dr. Abbas," he began, then moved through the whole game of hide and seek in that nebula, until *Sundering Wrath* had fled when Captain Boru got lucky.

"You think something similar here?" Abbas finally nodded.

"I think that *Doctor Kay* is not a warship ready to take on anything big," Maddox replied. "We've only got four missiles aboard, two Sixes and two Nines. Not enough to matter in a duel with another warship. Twin Particle cannon turret forward is probably a match for someone small. Maybe they only have one barrel. Plus, if they do try to run from us, I'm willing to gamble that we've got faster engines, so maybe we can run them down and bring them to justice. I need you folks telling me how we get there."

He sat back and watched the two glance at each other again. Surprise. Sure. Senoky had been a martinet who knew all the answers and was surrounded by imbeciles. All his reports had touched on those notes towards the end, when everything under Das had shown folks on a par with *Marrakesh*.

"Questions?" Maddox asked. Shaken heads. "Dismissed, then."

He would stay here, looking at maps of the vicinity.

At least until something happened.

THIRTEEN

Steve have gone beyond the forward cargo bay with his team. Into the space where the crew generally lived.

As he'd thought, two corridors forward, with this section largely divided into four columns as seen from above, but he was willing to bet that starboard would look just like port. And be just as abandoned.

"Porter, what have you got?" he asked as they tromped forward slowly on the magnets in their boots.

"Crew cabins and ship storage," Porter replied. "Laundry and pantry crap for the most part. Want me to look in any?"

"No," Steve replied. "Since we're without atmosphere here, I presume they are as well. We'll hit the bridge and see if we can get an intercom to work. Any chamber with air will resonate."

"Roger that," Porter said. "Vanya, you check the port side as we go. I'll watch starboard. That gets us there faster."

Steve nodded and fell in. He'd be watching the front, with Serge covering their asses as the other two touched the door controls along the bulkheads.

After a short run, Porter stopped.

"Squire, I've got the bridge here," he announced. "No atmosphere showing."

"Make entry and secure," Steve ordered him, looking around.

This part of the ship looked like it had landed somewhere and the crew wandered off. Like an empty vid set. No trash. No people.

No nothing.

Porter got the door open and Steve understood that they weren't going to find people.

Someone had opened fire in here with a Disruptor Bombardier on cyclic. Someone else had lobbed a few grenades into the space.

No dead bodies, but a lot of damage to just about every surface. And blood that has been flash-frozen by vacuum turns a particular color he'd never seen anywhere else.

"Bridge, you seeing this?" he asked.

"Affirmative, Perry," the Knight was suddenly on the line. "Did they make a last stand here, or did the pirates decide to shatter everything as they left? I have different response scenarios depending on your findings."

Perry grunted under his breath and followed Porter in.

Naval officers came in two flavors. Most of them went into some sort of flying service, ending up as pilots, engineers, or commanders. Something.

A few punks like him went into the close combat side instead. Every officer had some level of martial arts training, but only a handful made it their intended career. Like him.

It involved deep-diving into some of the more esoteric things, ground combat, among them. Survey Corps picked up a lot of his kind, because they were the ones that landed on strange worlds and walked around.

He studied the ebb and flow of the damage, then shifted over to this right.

"Serge, stop there, then shift to your left and look at the navigation station," Steve said.

He walked over to face Serge, then nodded.

"Porter, did they blow the lock controls on the hatch behind me?" Steve asked.

"Stand by," Porter said. "Yeah. Somebody hit it with a disruptor of some sort. Close range from the depth and splash. What have you got?"

"Somebody opened the same hatch we did," Steve replied, speaking clearly for the bridge to hear. "Firefight, with somebody standing about where I am, but crouched down. Didn't last long, because somebody put suppressing fire into the room, and someone else grenaded it. Then they swarmed, shooting everything that moved, including people knocked down. And not stun shots, from the amount of damage."

"Perry, this is Nevin," the CO said. "Confirm execution of prisoners?"

"Looks that way, sir," Steve replied, hearing the raw rage in the man's voice.

"Make sure you have good video evidence of everything to attach to your report, sailor," Nevin growled. "I want to make sure that we get to hang someone for this."

Steve nodded.

Some pirates tended to be pretty gentlemanly about it. Knock you down. Steal your cargo. Leave.

Others turned into mad dogs.

You didn't reason with those kinds. You put them down hard and considered the galaxy to be a better place afterwards.

"In process, Bridge," Steve replied. "We'll need some time

here, but the ship isn't going anywhere without some serious repair work."

"Understood, Perry," Nevin said. "Doubt that's our problem at this point, but I'll be sending a preliminary report to base in an hour or so and having them assign us our next task. You stay sharp, in case something comes up. Nevin out."

Steve nodded and turned to his team.

"Random sample of cabins, but I'm not expecting survivors or even bodies," he ordered. "Stay in teams of two. Porter and Vanya take starboard. Serge, you and I will sweep port. Go."

They weren't going to find anything.

Except evidence of a crime.

FOURTEEN

Narayana watched Nevin move. Fulminate. Control it with an iron will, but he was smoldering.

That gave Narayana a better insight into the man. Protector. Senoky had seen everyone else as beneath him. Peons to be ordered around, rather than people to be respected. A man who led from the back, instead of the front.

Maddox Nevin was more like Kumar Das. In good ways.

So far.

"Survey, what is your status?" Narayana asked on the intercom.

The pause was too long. Nevin looked over sharply and Narayana nodded. They'd seen something, but weren't sure.

"Sir, maybe you could come look at something?" Abbas asked in a sideways kind of voice.

"You handle that," Nevin said. "I'll take over here."

Narayana rose and Nevin slid into the command chair.

Aft, he found Abbas and Gammon leaned over a screen. They seemed surprised to see him instead of Nevin. Narayana smiled.

"What do you have?" he asked.

"We weren't coming in all that hot," Sabeen replied. "But we were watching our zone, because Nevin seemed worried that we'd get jumped."

"He's protecting the ship and crew in the middle of an unknown threat," Narayana replied automatically, then paused and considered his words.

They were almost as surprised as he was. But they nodded.

"Looking at our records, we did pick up some weird, stray signals that initially got logged as false positives," Sabeen continued.

"False?" Narayana asked.

"It happens," he nodded. "Especially when you crank up sensitivity as much as we did. Signals that don't make any sense to the computers get flagged for review, but in this case, they were so weird that they were marked lowest reliability. We'd have probably ignored them, if the Knight hadn't insisted on a review."

"What did you find?" Narayana asked, sharply intrigued.

"If, **IF** mind you, you were to crank your emissions way down," Sabeen said. "And maybe built some kind of baffle to disrupt the signal, it might be possible to slip into Ghost-space and maintain a decent rate of speed, while not being obvious about it. Stealthy. Won't let you run someone down, but a cargo ship probably isn't moving that fast anyway. Not invisible, but pretty damned hidden."

Narayana leaned back and thought about it, then turned to Chief Gammon. Not as smart or trained as Sabeen, but that left a lot of space for her to come close in many situations.

"You concur?" he asked.

"Affirmative," she said.

Narayana leaned in and dialed the number he wanted.

"Engineering. Forslund."

"Kjell, I'm with Sabeen in his office," Narayana said. "Turn things over to someone and join me."

"Be right there."

And he was, but they were already most of the way aft to Engineering already, because Survey had to supervise the VLS tools.

"What have you got?" Kjell asked as he entered.

"Look at this," Narayana said, sliding out of the way. "Sabeen, explain to him like you did me."

The room was crowded with four people, three standing. Normally, you sat two in here.

He listened to the explanation. Then the two of them—three when Chloe got involved—descended into a cant so dense that Narayana was lost, even with the decades he'd been doing this.

Kjell turned and scowled.

"Okay, assuming that it can be done, I think I know what I might try," Kjell said. "Dunno if it would work, but there aren't many ways to get a signal like that. You want me to build you something?"

"Reverse that," Narayana replied. "Assume they built it the way you'd do it. Tell us how to reconfigure our sensor array to see them anyway."

More scowl.

"Camden's probably better at that part," he finally admitted.

"Then pull her off duty and get her going on flights of fancy," Narayana nodded. "Our delicate Machinist probably needs that."

Kjell snorted.

"Delicate. Right."

They shared a grin. Camden Morgan was many things. Delicate was not one of them. Rugged. Opinionated. Smart. Even muscular, because she believed in hard work with her hands whenever possible.

Not delicate.

"How soon do you need it?" Kjell asked.

"Nevin will send a prelim report home in probably an hour," Narayana said. "If you and Camden can get me something, he can decide whether to include it. Otherwise, you and Sabeen work with her until she figures it out or decides that it's impossible."

"It's Camden," Kjell replied. "If I tell her something is impossible, she will move heaven and earth to prove me wrong."

"Yeah," Narayana chuckled. "I know."

FIFTEEN

It was crowded in the map room, but the only larger space was the patio on the top deck, only accessible while on the ground in an atmosphere.

Maddox had pulled the key players in for a briefing. About as well as he'd expected. Or as bad.

"So we're reasonably confident that they got away?" he asked, glancing back and forth between Yadav and Abbas. "At least for now?"

Squire Perry perked up at that, but Maddox wasn't surprised. That man had the same sort of opinion of predators as Maddox did.

"At least for now," Yadav replied, taking lead here like the Deck Officer was supposed to.

Protecting his people from a maniacal tyrant of a commanding officer. Or something.

"And we know the rough direction they fled?" Maddox pursued now, locking eyes with the Astronomer.

"Aye, sir," Abbas replied.

"What's over there?" Maddox asked simply, watching faces collapse into confusion.

Captain Boru had trained his people to plan out that extra step. To be prepared for that kind of question and have answers. It gave Maddox a direction to focus on, when trying to reach his new crew.

"Sir?" Abbas asked.

"If they went that way, and they weren't directly fleeing from us, since the vector is wrong, let's assume they had a reason," Maddox replied. "A base. A bolt hole. A friendly port. Something. They have cargo. We're confident from Perry that they didn't take prisoners, unless those fell into the category of pretty, young women, and we all know what that implies. I'm about to tell Fleet what we've found and ask for orders. I'd like to be able to offer suggestions. Like, maybe they send us after somebody. Or at least have us take a deeper look, if that's not a region anybody knows all that well."

Rather than answer, Yadav turned and pulled a binder down, laying it on the tabletop and flipping to the index. Then rifling around some.

He looked up, eyes on an invisible horizon.

"Assume our pirates are kinda lazy," Maddox said. "Maybe sail out to cause trouble, but want to be close to R&R facilities afterwards."

The others looked a bit confused, but the Deck Officer was supposed to be on top of these things. It was usually a promotion step to having your own boat, though Maddox had come way lateral and was in the process of saving this ship. At least he hoped so.

The crew had peculiar needs, and he had been working to understand them. And himself.

And learning.

"There is a place," Yadav said after flipping some more and turning the book around for Maddox to read.

Maddox looked at the notes.

Astarte III. Hithadhel Port on the surface. Astarte Station in orbit, but mostly a small trans-shipping and warehousing facility, rather than a base of any kind. Money was on the ground.

"Where's the line fall?" Maddox asked.

Rather than answer, Yadav pulled Abbas over and showed him.

The Astronomer did some quick math.

"Roughly twenty light-years at the closest approach, I think," the man replied.

"So a half day's sail into harbor?" Maddox asked.

"Maybe a day. Day and a half, sir," Abbas replied. "Short enough to make it an easy trip, but not close enough to be threatened. Or be seen on Aetherial Sensors if you made sure to introduce a dogleg in your course each direction."

"So a base out there somewhere?" Maddox asked.

"Basic repair and storage," Perry spoke up sharply. "Astarte III has everything you need for bigger and better. Including recruiting if you were careful."

Maddox locked eyes with the trooper. Noted the sharpness there.

"We've been through there, but not in a while," Perry said simply.

From the tone, Maddox assumed the last time they called on that port, Kumar Das was in command. It wasn't the place he'd been killed. That had been Aleyin.

Still, it was the sort of *Unaffiliated* world that Survey Corps liked to visit on a regular basis. Well beyond *A'Zedi*'s borders. It existed outside any areas claimed by others, because the region headed coreward was almost militantly independent, most of the time. Monsanch had been friendly, but Captain Boru had done them some major favors and become close friends with the governor.

"I'm going to play a hunch," Maddox told the group. "We'll file this report and wait for an answer or override, but I plan to tell them that our next port of call will be Astarte III. And why. Assuming nobody sounds recall, I need you and the crew sharp on what we know. And what we need to look for. Questions?"

He could see volumes of inquiries in their eyes, but everyone was still getting used to one another. Didn't know where he would draw that line and tear a kilo of flesh off somebody's ass for asking.

Something else he would need to break them of, however slowly.

Captain Boru had encouraged questions. Only way to learn.

Senoky had done the opposite. Before him, Inari Koser had been a by-the-books scholar who should have stayed with Fleet Operations instead of moving to Survey Corps.

"Dismissed," he said, when the silence stretched.

Abbas and Perry left. Yadav stayed behind.

"What do I need to know?" Maddox asked the man.

SIXTEEN

Narayana was still getting used to a boss who colored outside the lines. At least sometimes.

"Astarte III is a little more wild and wide open than some of the places you might have called previously," he replied diplomatically.

"As long as Perry's ready to cover the ship and the crew while we're on the ground, I'm not too worried," Nevin replied with a crisp nod. "Like I said, playing a hunch here, assuming that they didn't think they could be followed."

"Anything but a Survey ship paying close attention and you'd be right, sir," Narayana replied. "How will they react to us showing up?"

"I will presume that the locals aren't necessarily pirates themselves," Nevin said. "I plan to dig deep into the records we have once I send off my report. And request updates from them. If we can go safely, we'll pretend like we didn't see anything. Not like they would know who we were, since *Doctor Kay* was just a blip on Aetherials."

"And just poke around?" Narayana asked.

"That's up to Command," the man said. "When we get there, do we have any people we should or should not get involved on the ground?"

Narayana was again struck by the differences. Nevin reminded him more and more of Kumar. In good ways and bad. Ambitious, but generally well-tempered. Flexible when he needed, but willing to draw a hard line in the sand and enforce it.

Crew was still adjusting, but fewer and fewer disciplinary actions, once Narayana had dropped the boom a few times. Nothing Nevin had needed to know about.

"Perry's people all know the port," Narayana replied. "And some of the people. Hithadhel is pretty big, but the parts down towards the water are ship-focused. Highside folks generally stay away unless they have something they need. Pirates won't be up on the slopes, unless you're dealing with a boss or investor."

"And we'll be operating outside of any legal jurisdiction," Nevin nodded. "I don't want any trouble caused by us, but we also won't take any shit from anyone, either. If we can track them back to some base, then we'll see how big a hammer we need to call in to help up crack that nut."

Narayana nodded at that. Just exactly how Kumar would have done it. And the sort of thing that had gotten him killed.

Hopefully, he wasn't about to outlive another CO. From the things Nevin had hinted at, if something bad happened from here, they were likely to break up this entire crew and start over.

And he'd never see the stars from the deck of a warship again.

"Very good, sir," Narayana said. "Anything else?"

"No," Nevin said. "You see what we can do while I finish my report."

Narayana nodded and departed, back to the bridge next door where people were congregating perhaps more than was necessary.

"He serious about Astarte III?" Pretty asked quietly.

"Yes," Narayana replied. "Tell your people to be ready for ground operations, but low profile."

"Aye, sir," Pretty nodded, heading for the ladder down.

The troopers and most of the enlisted crew bunked on the lower deck. Perry preferred being with his people to having an officer's cabin on Main Deck. And trained with them.

It felt like they were going to need that shortly.

PART 2
ASTARTE III

SEVENTEEN

Maddox had the bridge, in spite of something like this normally being the provenance of the Deck Officer. It was both of their asses on the line with something like this, and Maddox wasn't taking chances today.

Kellogg was flying. Waters was handling Radio. Guns, what they were, were ready for anything, but he'd reminded everybody that *Doctor Kay* was too lightly armed for most trouble, unless he could stack the odds in his favor ahead of time.

Not like he hadn't done that a few times on *Marrakesh*.

Yadav was forward in a secondary control room, monitoring things for now.

"Kellogg, what is your status?" Maddox asked, loud enough that everyone could hear him.

She'd come to understand to answer just as loudly.

Keeping the bridge engaged.

"We'll come out of Ghost-space in thirty seconds, sir," she replied over her shoulder. "Showing nothing strange on my boards at present. The usual coming and going of ships, but nobody aimed at us or running the other direction."

"Be prepared to maneuver or run depending," he reminded her.

Then he waited.

Command had given him a lot of rope to follow up, based on the fuzzy guess of direction and possibilities. Plus, Astarte III wasn't someplace that got visited by *A'Zedi* vessels all that often anyway, so *Doctor Kay* was going to be updating a lot of records.

Their original mission, after all, had been to run an inspection tour of certain sensor buoys that were generally pointed at *Wronlori* space. All they were doing here was extending that out a couple of legs farther out into *Unaffiliated Space*.

The sort of world where they might have been traveling to next, anyway.

Best of play it cool, at least on the surface. And be prepared.

"Stand by to emerge," Kellogg called, then dropped them out of Ghost-space.

He'd told her to handle it by the books, rather than landing farther out like they might have wanted to. Totally innocent. Ignorant of any under-the-table goings-on around here, as it were.

Ship on a standard port call.

"Radio, anything exciting happening?" Maddox called after a few seconds.

"Light speed wave has crossed the planet's orbit," Waters replied. "Standard response from the computers, but I'm guessing that someone will wake up in a bit and ask more questions."

"Out sightseeing," Maddox reminded them. "I'll come up with a forward itinerary later, once we land and know what our next steps are."

Because nobody knew. Playing it by ear, instead of following orders to do things.

But that was also life in Survey Corps. *First In The Field.* Out looking for things, then deciding if he needed to call for help or run for his life.

And bring back a bigger hammer later.

"Okay, I'm getting live people," Waters called. "They want to know our landing preference."

Maddox considered.

Hithadhel Port had water docks as well as landing spaces, depending on your needs and configuration. *Doctor Kay* could handle both, but today he wanted land.

"Dry port, Waters," Maddox replied. "If available. Wet and docked if not."

"They have space, sir," Waters replied. "Putting us in for a landing space."

Maddox nodded. They'd likely be over with the bigger cargo vessels, because of their own size, rather than down with all the tramp freighters that hauled boxes between smaller worlds and stations in the closer light-years.

With any luck, one of those neighbors might even be a pirate, though Abbas hadn't been able to do anything that would let them identify a ship with a scan.

One step at a time.

"We have clearance for landing and a lane assignment," Waters called. "Kellogg, on your screen now."

"Confirm landing coordinates and lane assignment," she replied.

"Lock and engage, sailor," Maddox said.

As was beginning to be normal for her, the bob of the shoulders as she leaned forward and began typing. No questions. No complaints. Not waiting for exact details from him on how she was supposed to be doing her job, because of a CO who didn't think she did.

Get in and sail.

Maddox grinned and typed a number.

"Deck Officer," Yadav replied from his secondary station forward.

"It's Nevin," Maddox said. "Come aft and take over landing. I need to meet with the Coxswain and prepare for ground duties."

There was a longer pause than necessary.

"Be right there, sir," Yadav finally said.

Maddox grinned. Kellogg glanced back and caught it, confused for a moment before she grinned herself and went back to her station.

Narayana Yadav appeared quickly and they traded spots.

"Cox is below in his shop," Yadav offered quietly, also unprepared for the changes Maddox was introducing late in the game. "Anything I need to be prepared for?"

"Negative," Maddox smiled as he stood nearby. "Diplomat Vilchis will do her thing with all the officialness of her job. I plan on being a bit of a wildcard on the ground, just to see who flinches."

"Very good, sir," Yadav said, obviously lost, but willing to run with it for now.

Maddox made his way to the ladder and down, then forward to the Costume Shop.

Something else completely different from all his previous experience, but again, Survey Corps.

The Diplomacy Department, like all ship's departments including command, had two officers: Armiger Freya Vilchis as Diplomat and Squire Rolland Waters as Radio Officer. However, because Survey was responsible for going new places, and meeting new people, they also had a Costumer. In this case, Command Expert Jareth Laux, who also happened to be ship's Coxswain, or senior enlisted crew member.

Chief of the Boat, in many ways, but it always made Maddox shake his head to think about it.

He'd worn the *A'Zedi* mulberry and mauve for more than a decade now, and putting on civilian clothing these days felt alien to him. Especially since any leave he took usually involved staying on stations or other ships, where you never had to account for weather.

Laux looked up from his sewing machine as Maddox entered. There were robots you could program to turn out anything you needed from a catalog extremely quickly. The cloth was unrolled from the bolt, dipped in a starch to make it rigid, and then the machines went to work.

Laux, as Maddox had seen, liked to keep his fingers nimble.

Presumably, he would eventually retire eventually and get a job as a fashion designer. Or something.

Man had nearly thirty years in service, and was old enough, barely, to be Maddox's dad, depending. He looked like a professional weightlifter rather than a tailor. Like he should be on Perry's security team, but Maddox knew that he'd been in Diplomacy for his whole career.

Man just liked sewing.

"Sir?" Laux asked when Maddox entered.

"Ground operations, Cox," Maddox said simply. "I need a uniform for walking around the city in the current climate."

"Rainy season, commander," the man said automatically. "Overcoat or cloak?"

Maddox had to stop and consider that. Technically, both were allowed, but the latter was far less common.

"How windy is it out?" he asked.

"Monsoons should be another month or two out," Laux said. "Dry season high winds in the winter. Calm and wet now. You should be fine for a week or two."

"Do me a cloak?" Maddox asked.

Laux studied him for a long moment, then surprised Maddox by standing from his machine and walking over to a cubbyhole on one wall, where he rifled through stacks of cloth for a moment and pulled something out.

"Made it for Das," he said. "Man only wore it once. You two are about the same size."

Maddox took it from Laux's hands almost reverently. He figured that he must have come up in the world for a gift like this, as he'd been expecting Laux to make him something on the fly. It would look good, but when he unfolded this one, it was amazing.

Mulberry lined with mauve, as was to be expected. Officers normally had silver stripes on their shoulder boards or epaulets. Here, Laux had worked in three stripes on both collarbones, hip to opposite shoulder in alignment.

"Put it on so I can check," Laux ordered.

Maddox did, marveling at the fit. To the middle of his calves, with pockets inside to hold things and buttons where he could close it in a breeze.

Warm. Must have lined it with something.

He wondered if he should ask for an armored version of some sort. A layer inside that might slow a disruptor bolt or something.

"Yup," Laux said, walking around. "You and Knight Das were almost exactly the same height, but you've got more shoulders. Not enough to matter, as most of your bulk is chest, but I don't figure you'll get a pissy admiral with a tape measure inspecting you. And I'll have it fixed by then."

"What have you got in civilian?" Maddox asked.

The man's face collapsed.

"Sir?"

"I might want to walk around out of uniform somewhere, Cox," Maddox smiled. "Be handy if I had the gear for it. My previous captain went undercover a few times."

Okay, stretching it, but Monsanch had been an adventure for Captain Boru, right up to the point Maddox and a bunch of security troopers had rescued him from being kidnapped.

"Give me a day, sir," Laux finally caught up. "Body guards, too?"

"At least one," Maddox agreed. "Maybe all of Perry's people need low profile garb."

"That, they have," Laux replied, warming to his subject. "Did you need anything in particular, or just civilian?"

"Middle-class local," Maddox suddenly decided, thinking back to the briefing notes and conversations with Perry. "If I get invited anywhere fancy, I'll be in uniform. Same if I have to kick in a door somewhere with disruptor bombardiers in hand."

Laux blinked, then nodded.

"We'll be ready by tomorrow," he said.

"Excellent," Maddox smiled. "Thank you."

"All hands, stand by for atmospheric maneuvering," Yadav announced over the intercom, so they were ready to make their descent.

Maddox nodded to Laux and made his way back up to the main deck. He'd ride this one in the map room, like he did most things, with his new cloak slung over one arm.

They were here. Things were about to get interesting.

EIGHTEEN

Maddox smiled and didn't let Yadav's sourness deflect him.

"Because it needs doing, and Headquarters is still looking for any reason to get you in trouble, Narayana," Maddox explained. Again. "Armiger Vilchis will do her thing. Meanwhile, I want to get some sort of feel for the town."

"The Sabine Star might not be the safest place to start, sir," his Deck Officer grumbled.

"That's why I'm taking Perry," Maddox nodded. "And why you will have the rest here, save for whoever is sent with Vilchis, in case we need a flying column to rescue us from whatever trouble might think to bother me in town. And that is my final word."

Yadav swallowed his grumbles. Maddox had gotten pretty good at reading the man. And understanding him.

Still, Hithadhel wasn't any place Maddox had ever been. And if they were supporting piracy, even tangentially, he needed to know more. Squire Perry had been here a while back. As has Serge Broom, though he didn't talk much about it, even when asked.

Must have been good.

"Very good, sir," Narayana nodded. "Try not to cause me any heartburn while you're out?"

"That's my intention," Maddox grinned. "You hold the fort here."

He moved past the man and ascended the conning tower. *Doctor Kay* could land on water, then use thrusters to move about, in which case there was a control station up here that could be manned. Similarly, watch would be kept, water-borne or ground, because Maddox didn't want strangers meandering too close to his hull without a damned good reason.

Up top, he found Perry. *Pretty*, though again, he didn't use that name to his face. Not yet. Not until everyone was more comfortable.

They were getting there. That was the whole point of this first sail.

Wasn't the same as arriving.

Weather was a heavy damp that felt colder than the meteorological section had suggested. No rain, but it threatened it. Four degrees, but felt like freezing anyway.

Maddox slipped on his cool new cloak and checked that he had a Type Three Personal Disruptor slipped into a pants pocket against need. Not obvious. Not threatening.

Perry had an Adjustable Disruptor on one hip, with a long-coat unbuttoned so he could get to it quickly.

Of course, Perry also looked tougher than the weather. Meaner, too.

As long as the walk to a bus station wasn't too great.

Lots of walking on Astarte III. They had skycars, but not a lot of them, and folks walked or took buses. Or had small boats they could use to get around the harbor, because almost all of what you might need for supplies or entertainment backed up to the water's edge.

Kalyn Blackford was on dry land. Not far from the nearer edges of the landing reservation, so only about a kilometer walk to the nearest gate. The ship didn't have any ground vehicles aboard and he had specifically decided to walk anyway.

"We ready?" he asked Perry, looking up at the man.

"Waiting for you, sir," Perry smiled.

Maddox nodded and headed down the ramp.

Graveled ground was damp but not wet. Sky threatened rain, but had only drizzled over the last few hours they'd been down.

Early morning, Hithadhel Port City.

Maddox wanted to see the city from the ground. He'd already overflown it and memorized maps.

What were the people like?

NINETEEN

Maddox wasn't entirely sure how to describe the place, beyond big. One building. Too low to be a sports stadium. One high part of a roof over a concert hall, but only back in that one corner. The rest covered several hectares, all under one cover, no matter how much it changed pitch and height. Looked like one building that had been expanded. Then added onto. Then again.

Then some more.

"That's the place?" he asked Perry.

Rhetorically, because it was the biggest building in town. Possibly on the planet, because they didn't have all that much formal government on Astarte III.

Perry grinned.

The Sabine Star.

According to the notes he'd reviewed, they had every option for entertainment someone had figured out how to make a profit from, ranging from a brothel to a library. And damned near every stop in between.

Perry had brought them in from what felt like the dockside

entrance, rather than the big landing field out front for skycars and shuttles. More like sailors coming to get their coals raked and their wallets emptied. Middle of the morning, so probably staggering back to their ships.

Hopefully there was a harbor patrol to keep semi-drunks from drowning.

Unaffiliated world, but they took *A'Zedi* ducats as well as *Wronlori* Marks. And probably everything else. Felt far more cosmopolitan than he'd originally been expecting.

Good, and bad.

More likely that pirates might call on a place like this regularly. Which generally meant that the locals were less likely to be helpful to a passing Survey Corps vessel. He wasn't the cops here. Wasn't entirely sure what role he filled, because even the notes he'd read were a little iffy on the topic.

Still, he was here. Armiger Vilchis was going to City Hall to call on the Mayor, because that was covered in the briefing notes.

Maddox was a free agent for now. Later, that would likely change, but nobody knew he was here yet.

Except the younger woman eyeing him speculatively from behind a lectern nearby as they entered the complex. Just inside the door Maddox found a courtyard. Or something. Covered, but big. Perry nodded in her direction, so Maddox went.

Bistro Himilco was the sign over her head, but he had no idea what the name referred to. Still, bistro made sense. As did the smells.

"Knight...?" she asked as he got close to the lectern she was standing at.

Hiding behind, maybe. Small woman. Lighter skin than Maddox's.

"Maddox Nevin," he replied automatically, looking at her

and the place behind her. "*A'Zedi* vessel *Doctor Kalyn Black-ford*. Just landed."

"Ah," she nodded. "Wondered who that was. Welcome to Bistro Himilco. First visit to Astarte?"

"It is," he replied. "My crew suggested this was a good place to get food, while I waited for the local structure to acknowl-edge my Diplomat."

She nodded like she understood *A'Zedi* military proce-dures and grabbed two menus, leading them deeper into the space.

Low ceilings and dim made it feel homey. Corridor down the center with meter-high half-walls divided the space into a restaurant on the left and a kitchen with a bar wrapped around on the right, with seating close enough that the cooks could deliver your plates themselves. Kinda what he'd expect from a sushi place, but not this.

Still, the smells were lovely. And both sides were almost completely empty.

She led them to a booth and got them settled, though Perry balked for about a half-second because he wanted to stand guard until Maddox scowled the man into motion.

"Can I get you something?" she asked.

"Coffee for me," Maddox replied.

"Hot tea with lemon and honey," Perry said, the look on his face daring Maddox to comment.

She left them alone. Perry watched the place like an angry raptor. Maddox studied the kitchen.

On a ship, the kitchen was always packed as tightly as it could get, usually with a window they could slide troughs of food out as things got done. Efficient. Not performance art, which was what this place promised, from the way the half-walls seemed to emphasize the cooks instead of hiding them.

The young woman disappeared past the kitchen through a hatch. A middle-aged man emerged on her heels a few moments later, looking this way and nodding.

A waitress brought drinks, then flinched when a man came up behind her. She slid off to one side like a mouse surrounded by cats.

"Gentlemen," the man said. "Scott Hysmith. Owner of the Bistro Himilco and principle chef. We don't often get *A'Zedi* naval officers in town. What can we do for you this morning?"

Perry was in uniform as a Squire. Maddox was a Knight. He supposed that they might look important. Or at least intimidating.

"My CO's never been to Astarte," Perry suddenly said. "I recommended this place, from when you first opened two years ago on my first mission in space."

"Oh?" Hysmith replied, eyes growing vague as he searched for some memory. "Two years? Corvette *Blackford*?"

"The same, sir."

Perry seemed impressed. Maddox was.

"Back on a new patrol run?" Hysmith asked.

It sounded innocent. Maddox was playing it safe.

"Extended shakedown cruise," Maddox replied. "Spend some time in port here making sure everything is working correct, then circle back on a different arc from the one we came in."

Nothing sensitive from an intelligence standpoint, save that they might be here for a week or two, depending, but Vilchis was already going to be telling the Mayor those sorts of things, and it would get out.

"Well, it's a bit late for breakfast and early for brunch, but I'm certain we can get you lads taken care of," Hysmith beamed. "Welcome to Himilco."

He stepped back and gestured the waitress to step back up, then withdrew to the kitchen and put on an apron, the cook already in place watching with a bemused face.

Then they were alone.

"Did we make that big a splash, last time?" Maddox asked.

"Maybe," Perry shrugged. "This joint was just in the process of a soft opening, and Knight Das was a bit of a gourmand, so we ate here a few times. Must have made a good impression."

"Hope so," Maddox replied. "He's cooking for us."

"I saw that," Perry grinned. "He was damned good last time."

Maddox nodded and settled in to watch the place. Almost empty, but again, that stretch of morning after the first rush of folks had gone to work and before the ones who had slept in had crept out.

A starship is always on duty. Always working, around the clock.

Hithadhel Port was on the surface of a planet, so he could see it adjusting to daylight and darkness. Still, ports ran similar schedules, based on when ships came and went. Mostly arrived, as you could take off whenever you wanted to depart but landing was a lot easier with sunshine.

And he was only playing a hunch that those pirates had come this way, based on it being close enough to the line they had initially fled from *Doctor Kay*.

What would they find here?

TWENTY

Maddox burped as they exited the bistro. And smiled. It had been amazing. And Hysmith had come back over after they finished eating, mostly to chat.

Catch up on news from *A'Zedi*. Gossip about innocuous things around here.

Friendly.

One hoped.

They were still inside The Sabine Star, but it covered an entire square kilometer. Maddox decided to wander. Perry looked as much as much like an aide as a bodyguard, and someone might mistake him thus, though Maddox did see occasional goons that looked like bouncers or deputies as he walked.

Shopping mall as he went deeper. Dozens of shops, each focused on some aspect of life in space, even on the surface of a planet. This establishment was focused on sailors from the looks of everything.

Just past the mall part, two meter neon signs indicated the Sabine Star portion of the facility. Maddox watched the grand foyer of the brothel as he and Perry meandered closer. Bar down one side. Tables with a few card games going on the other. Not a lot of people at present, but it was coming up on an early lunch, depending on the local culture, and he supposed that this might be a lull time.

At least he hoped so. There hadn't been a lot of foot traffic around them, but some. Seventy-five percent male, but a majority of sailors tended to be, so he wasn't surprised.

Looking at the front, he was again surprised. Much higher quality than he'd been expecting. Obviously, extremely profitable.

He'd seen places where things were...a bit further down the socio-economic scale, as it were.

A woman caught his eye and gestured him closer. Maddox shrugged and complied.

He was here to learn more about Astarte III and Hithadhel Port. He supposed that this might be the heart and perhaps soul, since this segment appeared to be the original Sabine Star for which the entire complex was named.

How much money had they made?

"Knight," she said as he stepped close, inclining her head.

Maddox matched it. Perry did, a moment later.

"Is there a particular service we can offer you, sir?" she asked, eyes glittering with interest.

"I've been on the ground for about five hours," Maddox replied. "And never visited this system before."

"Did you have anywhere you needed to be?" she asked, stepping close and turning, but stymied in her attempt to grab his elbow because he'd left the cloak down as he walked.

Maddox studied the woman. As tiny as he was tall. Maybe a meter and a half. If that. Delicate and slender in spite of that.

Almost ethereal. Hair dyed a platinum blonde because her eyebrows were still brown. Attractive.

He flipped his cloak back, laughing to himself at how dramatic it probably looked to outsiders. Still, she took his elbow with a knowing grin and guided him into that grand foyer with thick red carpet underfoot and art on the walls. Ornate scrollwork on the dark-stained wood and bar.

Sailors and locals, but dressed nicer than civilian sailors normally were. No uniforms other than he and Perry, but Yadav hadn't seen any other military vessels in orbit or on the ground, local gendarmes and search-and-rescue boats notwithstanding.

"Stefana Davidovich," she introduced herself. "The manager."

"Are you the Sabine Star?" Maddox asked as she guided him to a table and get them settled.

"Oh no," she smiled and shook her head. "That would be my boss, Asya Orlova, who owns this entire operation."

"I have just come from breakfast at Himilco," Maddox nodded. "From here, I'm told that I needed to tour this entire facility, mostly to see the sights."

"Certainly," she nodded. "Whatever your needs, we can accommodate them. Something to drink?"

Maddox considered the mass of food slowly digesting in his belly. Really good food.

"Some Irish coffee, perhaps?" he asked, turning to Perry, who also nodded.

One, and they'd be fine. The regulations did not forbid drinking alcohol on duty. They covered situations where you were rendered unfit for duty **due** to drink.

And he suspected that he had a full day ahead of him,

though at present Maddox had no intentions of visiting the brothel part of whatever this was.

"Excellent, gentlemen," she bounced up. "Right away."

And she was gone.

Maddox turned to Perry. And noted that man was physically capable of blushing, though he'd have never known it prior to this.

"Previous visit," Perry said, tight-lipped. "Shore leave for the crew after a long sail."

Maddox nodded. A smart commanding officer let the crew blow off steam from time to time, just as he tightened the screws down others. The key was doing so with transparency and predictability.

If he was here enjoying himself, he should make accommodations for the crew to do the same.

As long as nobody got arrested, he didn't have to notice officially.

Davidovich returned with two mugs of steaming coffee quickly, setting them down and joining them at the round table with a bright smile.

Maddox supposed he looked like a stack of ducats to her. Especially if he had a full crew that might have needs and time ashore.

"What brings you to Astarte?" she asked brightly. Leadingly.

Maddox ended up giving her almost the exact same story as he had Hysmith earlier, understanding just how small this town probably was.

They would need to make sure that any sailors going ashore understood to remain quiet about the freighter *Livingston* and that situation. At least for now.

Sin of omission, as it were.

"And we cannot entice you?" she asked, an easy and obvious tease that was as much automatic as professional.

The manager of a brothel, talking to a pair of young naval officers new in town.

A story as old as stories, Maddox supposed.

"I'm likely to be spending significant time overseeing the ship and anything that came loose on this first voyage out of a full drydock," Maddox grinned. "Once we have a handle on that, I'm at the mercy of my own commanders as to when I must depart. The plan is to free some crew up for short leave, once we know how the mayor will react."

"I can't see her having any issues," Davidovich replied with a knowing smile. "Skye Thoran is owned almost entirely by the local business collective, and hardly ever bucks that set of taskmasters."

Maddox nodded and filed that away. Common in many places, where money was power and a Mayor was frequently a figurehead emplaced to make certain that the wealthy of the district weren't bothered.

It also suggested that the Sabine Star was probably closer in power to a planetary governor than most folks appreciated. He'd update his notes once he knew more.

"And a gentle reminder that the Sabine Star also hosts more conversational events," Davidovich offered. "Geisha, performing and entertaining. Additionally, dinner theater events on the weekends, frequently catered by Mr. Hysmith's staff. Truly, the limits are your imagination."

She said that with just enough emphasis and body language to suggest that even his imagination might not be sufficient. Or that she might be on the menu if he asked nicely.

Maddox had been on duty for a decade, between uni, service, and the war. Now, with an independent command as well. He'd never really had time to work on finding a wife and settling down, unlike some officers.

And Captain Boru had shared a few thoughts about his previous few boyfriends. Not everyone was cut out to be involved long-term with a sailor. There were long voyages away from home, followed by short, intense reunions. Then separation again.

He could see how professionals willing to offer the illusion of intimacy could make a tremendous profit in a short time. After that, they might marry sailors. Or local farmers.

Or take over the entire economy of some world and build themselves a business empire.

"I shall keep all that in mind," Maddox deflected nicely.

She allowed herself to be deflected, then parted with a few words and smiles, leaving he and Perry alone in a vast space with just enough music playing to cover most conversations.

"Still good?" he asked his bodyguard.

Perry nodded, eyes still watching the room and everyone in here.

Maddox supposed that he might be introduced to life at the higher echelons around here, based on who and what he was.

At the same time, he had a mission, and the need to find out primarily if his unknown pirates ever called here.

And maybe how to catch them.

TWENTY-ONE

Narayana had done the usual babysitting in port. Kumar had frequently gone ashore and left the old man in charge, so Nevin's behavior wasn't all that different.

How much had Nevin known about Kumar Das? Or had command found another commander in the same mold for the ship? And what did that say?

Because Nevin had established it as something of a habit, Narayana was working in the Map Room, with the hatch open in case someone had a need. Perry's people were up on the conning tower keeping watch. The rest of the ship was generally shut down for maintenance and cleaning, since even life support could be turned off right now and taken apart.

A shadow and a knock drew his attention.

"Joy," he said as she stepped into the room. "News?"

Shipfitter Joy Kimmel. Armiger. Hull officer. Nerd, who built musical instruments by hand in her spare time, having made certain that she had enough space allotted for personal gear to cover it.

"We finished the inventory of *Livingston*'s various cargo

bays," she said, sitting across the table from him. "Took a while, because they didn't do a good job of inventory assessment and we didn't stay long enough to actually count everything."

"But?" Narayana prompted.

"But we know what was stolen with a ninety percent probability," she acknowledged.

Ninety was high from her. She was also a perfectionist on those sorts of things.

Narayana waited expectantly.

"Mostly, machine parts," she nodded. "Industrial stuff intended for power stations. But hold number three also had a lot of commercial gear for starship repair."

"Do tell?" he asked, intrigued.

"Imagine if someone put in an order to restock a repair shop," she replied. "Not a yard, where they buy things in big lots or machine them on site. The place you go where they have some of the more common replacement parts that a tramp freighter needs for general overhaul and maintenance."

"We got model numbers?" Narayana pressed.

"Mostly manufacturers," she countered. "A lot of stuff that's generally standard across entire lines of ships. One kind of life support generator, for instance. Auxiliary power units that fit a standard bracket and can be installed with hand tools."

"Civilian stuff," he noted.

"Agreed," she said. "*A'Zedi*. Obvious, given the location. Being hauled to coreward worlds. Or someone that had a chain of parts shops. Townsend Power Industrial is the manufacturer. They do a lot of gear for folks like Bradford Stellar, Garza Group Of Athanak, and Galloway Fabritronics."

"Work with Vilchis and Waters," he ordered. "See how many of those kinds of ships we scanned in the vicinity."

"You expecting them to dump stuff here?" She seemed surprised. "This quickly?"

"If they thought someone saw them, they might have figured we'd spend a while on the wreck," he said. "Or returned to our usual patrol when it was obvious there was nothing for us to do. Nevin just pushed us in a particular direction."

"He good, or just lucky?" she asked. "Haven't spent that much time with the man."

"Both," Narayana sobered. "Trying to get that to rub off on us."

"In that case, let me go bother Adrian Stevens, too," Joy said, rising. "Since she handles a lot of quartermaster stuff, she might be the kind of person we sent into town for weird stuff. Oh, hey, I have an idea. Not sure how well Nevin would go for it, though."

"Talk to me," Narayana said.

"Standard parts, you know?" she asked, waiting for him to nod. "What if we made up some bullshit story about needing one of those non-factory-standard APUs for something on the ship? We've got serial numbers from the wreck, because they're big and expensive enough to track individually. If we bought one, we could see where it came from."

"You and Adrian work that out, but don't say anything yet," he replied. "The Knight will need to give his blessing. Plus, what would you do with such a thing?"

"Dunno," Joy grinned. "Maybe mount it in Boyce's cargo bed so she could provide excessive power in the field or on the ground. They aren't that big or heavy. Just awkward. But we never have enough power around here."

"Then ask Forslund to get involved, too," Narayana said, suddenly feeling like this had gone from a simple task to a major project.

"On it," she said, departing and leaving him to stew.

On the one hand, it would get almost every department involved, directly or not. But Maddox Nevin might not go for it, once the scale became obvious. And the officers were all solid, rumor and innuendo notwithstanding, but some of the enlisted were still a little bitey after going feral for so long.

How did he convince the new guy that they could all be trusted?

TWENTY-TWO

Maddox had walked back to the ship with the cloak's hood up, staying dry and toasty in the drizzle. Perry had pulled a crush hat from a pocket and jammed it on his head, but it hadn't done much.

"You shower and get warm," Maddox ordered him pointedly when they got back inside where it was warm. "Then spend an hour or two writing up all your observations from this morning's operation. I'll do the same, but we saw different things, and I want to assemble one big list before we update the crew and let folks start taking shore leave."

"Aye, sir," Pretty replied grumpily.

Maddox just smiled and headed into the Map Room, unsurprised to find Yadav sitting there.

He fixed himself some coffee and gestured Narayana to stay in place, then joined him.

"You look like a man selling mining claims to strangers just off the shuttle," Maddox offered, mostly to watch Narayana's eyes cross as he parsed that.

"Maybe?" Yadav offered. "You want me to talk first, or you?"

"I didn't do anything exciting, except to get fed and entertained by various locals," Maddox laughed. "Good breakfast. The brothel is something to behold, even if all you do is drink coffee in the front room, like we did. The bookstore was interesting. The arcade a little too loud for my tastes. The sweet shops might do a roaring business until we can convince the Supply Department to relax inventory standards enough for random cookies."

"That's the Purser," Narayana replied. "Armiger Buccheri has always taken himself a little too seriously. He actually got along swimmingly with Senoky."

The way he said it put a bigger smile on Maddox's face. His Deck Officer was coming around. And a good Purser was like that, counting every ducat and farthing, while also maintaining payroll records for the entire crew, so they could draw cash for shore leave.

Like now.

And maybe Maddox would see about getting a different Purser at some point. Though he was definitely keeping Squire Grippen and Senior Expert Cordell Llewellyn to manage cooking. Damned good food.

"You talk," Maddox said, sipping more coffee.

It had been a cold, wet, dreary, coffee kind of day out there.

"It starts with Kimmel, and branches out to most of the ship," Yadav replied. "She thinks that we might offer to buy a particular model of APU from the local chandlers, then see if it matches serial numbers with stolen stock when we take possession."

Maddox paused and did the math. All that made sense. Except...

"What do we do with a spare APU?" he asked. "Keep it and sell it later?"

"She suggested putting it in Boyce's shuttle as a portable generator station," Yadav countered.

"We could do that," Maddox said. "What if we went ahead and built some sort of land vessel and used the APU to power it? Something that could be broken entirely down in transit and reassembled on site. Same, maybe, with a boat. We have the inflatables, but they wear out over time. What if we had a permanent boat and a permanent truck we could assemble, neither taking up that much space aft?"

He liked the way Narayana considered that.

"Honestly, I don't know how big it is," the man admitted. "But she's going to talk to Forslund. Maybe we include her and have her and Calder do some design work?"

"That's on you, Deck Officer," Maddox grinned. "I'm pretty sure I just need to sign off on purchases, otherwise."

"Something like that, sir," Yadav said.

"Will it work?" Maddox asked, cutting through all the bullshit to get to the heart of the matter.

"I've been sitting here thinking about it, sir," Narayana replied. "And it has most of the pieces. What I don't have is any confidence in the players involved to know if we can pull off this level of stupidity without being caught."

"If nothing else, we can always request that Astarte III be removed from our sailing orders for a while," Maddox told him. "At least until most of the current officers move on. What would make you more confident?"

"Honestly, sir?" Yadav asked.

Maddox paused him with a gesture, then reached back and closed the hatch, just in case anyone was on the nearby bridge listening.

"Was that necessary?" his Deck Officer asked.

"Maybe."

"More confidence from me would be an understanding of where you expect this ship and crew to sail, at least metaphorically."

Maddox nodded at that.

"All of you hated Senoky," Maddox replied, waiting for the nod. "Most of you, anyway. I don't particularly like him, and we've never met. Option One, we present to the locals that I'm just as bad, but I don't think that works because it blows your cover almost immediately."

"What doesn't?" Narayana asked.

"What if I'm a cowboy here?" Maddox asked. "You and I have spoken a bit about some of my adventures on *Marrakesh*, but not gone too deeply because of security classification issues and some of your background that we don't need to rehash right now, Narayana Yadav."

He paused, noting how serious the man had grown.

"When I took the transfer and the lateral, I was interviewed by some extremely senior people on what *First In The Field* means," Maddox continued. "To me, it frequently means coloring outside the lines, because there might not be any lines here. I'm okay with that, if I can rely on the crew to lock down as pros when shit starts to go sideways. And it will. Nature of the beast and the service. If you need to buy or even steal an APU from somewhere because you need a new ground vehicle or boat or even helicopter for your crazy commanding officer, go for it. I'll back you there, because I can see where it works to our advantage later. And if it gets us leads on the pirates, I probably have to take point there, because the folks involved will all be pretty big players. Nobody a mere Squire would be talking to on a daily basis.

Again, you find me the leads. My job will be to track it down, kill it, and drag it back to the fire for you to clean it and cook it. We good so far?"

He paused. Yadav seemed to be having a crisis of conscience, but got over it pretty quickly.

"It might involve risk," Yadav countered.

"This job is risk, sailor," Maddox said bluntly. "It got Kumar Das killed in one of those random events that is the blackest swan possible, leaving his crew with a pair of dipshit commanders after that. I want you people back to winning awards regularly for style and professionalism. Right now, that looks to me like I'm tracking down some sort of pirate ring so we can figure out what we need to do to smash it later. Am I wrong?"

"You are not," Narayana said. "About any of it."

"Then do it, and tell me what my part needs to be here," Maddox said. "The crew relies on you as Deck Officer. I'm just the latest idiot CO of this boat. You run it. You tell me where to go and who to talk to to pull this off."

Poor fellow looked like he'd swallowed a live frog, but Maddox merely smiled at his discomfort.

"Helicopter?" Narayana asked after a time. "Isn't a shuttle more useful?"

"Helicopter rides on rotating blades that generate lift," Maddox nodded. "Hard to pick someone up on thrusters without scorching them in the process. Primitive, I know, but I figured it's not much worse than a speedboat or a truck that we can assemble. Perry certainly got to walk a lot more than he might be used to today, time on treadmill notwithstanding."

"And you'll let me run it?" Yadav asked. "Just like that?"

"Just like that," Maddox agreed. "I need this crew. You need this crew. This gets us there. You have all the pieces and know the sailors. I'm learning who the locals are and can wave a big flag in front of them as a distraction as needed."

Maddox watched, then grinned.

"Not the day you were expecting?" he asked.

"Not even remotely, sir," Narayana agreed.

"Let's see if we can do that to them, too," Maddox smiled.

He rose and took his coffee with him. His quarters weren't far away, but he could be off duty and let his people sort it out on their own.

He was the wildcard here, after all.

How could he use that the most effectively?

TWENTY-THREE

Narayana sat and just thought for twenty minutes before rousting his butt off the chair, mostly to let the shock wear off. Nevin might go for it. Might turn out to be the leader this crew needed to get back to what they'd been before.

Maybe.

Standing, he headed aft first, not surprised to find Joy and Kjell—the division officers—talking heatedly with their Squires, Machinist Camden Morgan and Repair Officer Astrid Calder. Neither of their chiefs were here, so it was an officer conversation for now.

Usually the most dangerous kind.

His appearance caused all of them to stutter.

Narayana smiled and closed the hatch behind him.

That just made the ominous silence worse, but he might be stretching things a bit. Not like he didn't owe all of them a thing or two.

"I've just spoken with the Knight," he announced in one of those tones that got their undivided attention.

"And?" Joy asked when he stopped.

"He's in," Narayana nodded. "Buy or steal an APU and he'll approve it. He suggested that we add a collapsible helicopter to the other options, when you get to designing something for an APU to power."

"Shit," Camden muttered. "Really?"

"Really," Narayana grinned. "Worse, he suggested that he'll have to play the role of adventurer, if we do find something, so make sure we keep him protected. Pirates are likely to want to cover their backtrail, especially if we start sniffing."

"That's probably Serge," Kjell noted. "Pretty stands out too much to be undercover, but Broom can vanish in an empty room."

"Agreed," Narayana replied. He turned to Camden. "You and Joy identify the APU models that freighter carried, then design me a system for it, as compact and portable as possible. If we're ordering the one, include whatever other parts we need to acquire, either electronics or things we can machine, because I doubt that they'll be in stock."

"Tiltrotor," Kjell said absently.

"What the hell is that?" Narayana countered.

"Helicopter, but you can turn the blades forward to fly really fast," he replied.

"Whatever," Narayana said. "I need a solid enough design that enemy mechanics just nod when told about it. And plans that we can show someone if they get tetchy. Questions?"

"What's Nevin going to do in this situation?" Joy asked.

"Back us," Narayana told her. "That was his promise just now. Whatever we needed to pull off this con effectively. Whatever he needed to do in town to distract the local power players from getting too close to what we're up to."

"He's nuts," she muttered.

"He's trying to keep us employed," Narayana rasped,

pausing to look over his shoulder, but the hatch was closed and secured. "Sit, all of you."

Kids. He had a decade and a half on Joy as the oldest. Two on Camden. Days like this, Narayana felt all of his years in service. But they'd been good years, and Kumar had bent every regulation and called in every favor and blackmail that he could in order to get Narayana Yadav back in space.

He owed Kumar everything. And this crew.

"Something Nevin told me under strictest confidence, so if you repeat it, we probably all get court martialed and tossed in the stockade forever. Okay?"

He waited for nods.

Frightened looks, which was good. They hadn't done the math on commanding officers like he had.

"Command assigned us Nevin," he continued. "And he's mentioned to me that he was interviewed by extremely senior people ahead of this. Like Marshals and such, when normally a Sector Captain might be it. Do I have your attention?"

Oh, he had it. Sharp as a razor.

"You—WE—broke two previous Knights because they weren't Kumar Das," he reminded them. "Didn't measure up to the boss we all loved. Command probably looked at this situation and flipped a coin. Either they assign us Maddox Nevin and hope he can pull it off, or they decide that we've gone sour and they need to break the entire crew up and assign us to different boats. Those of us not permanently grounded. Nevin has played it straight with me. And I know he has done the same with you. Now, I need all of you to put your shit back in the footlocker and start acting like sailors. Same with your departments. No more horseplay. No more bullshit. We're hunting down pirates and might actually manage to find them, if nobody fucks this up. Nevin is willing to run point for you, when you and I both know that he probably has to look over his shoulder far more than he ought to as commanding officer. As Deck Officer, I'm drawing a line, right here, right now. We are officers in the *A'Zedi* navy. We need to act like it. Am I clear?"

He leaned back because he'd hunched forward, weight on his toes. Angry. The others remembered to breathe after a few moments.

Finally, nods.

Camden hesitated, then spoke.

"I can design whatever I want?" she asked timidly.

Camden? Timid? Good, he had her attention.

"As long as it will work," he replied. "And can be broken down later for storage without compromising Boyce's space."

He looked around.

"What do you need from me?" Narayana asked.

"Adrian Stevens," Joy said. "I can brief her, but you'll need to reinforce that pretty heavy. She can be a troublemaker, more by accident than design, and gets into places she shouldn't, sometimes has equipment she shouldn't, and doesn't mind doing a little back-room trading now and then. Probably exactly what this situation requires."

Narayana nodded.

"You get her prepped while Camden goes to work," he ordered. "Then send her to me. Also, any sailor who goes ashore will be under strict orders not to mention that derelict we found, so start a list of folks who are sloppy drunks and can't get leave until we sort this out. We haven't been at sea long enough to be trouble, so shore leave will be a reward for good behavior instead of a relief valve, and plan it that way. Also, I need your lists of everything that still needs to be tightened, loosened, or replaced, plus associated parts, if Camden is making a list and Stevens is going shopping. We good?"

Nods. Fear of God nods, but this ship probably needed that. They'd been coasting for too long. Too obstreperous.

Time to act like sailors again.

"Keep me posted," Narayana said as he moved to the exit.

TWENTY-FOUR

Expert Sailor Adrian Stevens hadn't been to Astarte III in years, but she didn't figure it had changed that much. Regulations were also a bit fuzzy on whether or not she needed to go into town in uniform or civilian mufti doing this, so she'd gone for something green and low-key.

Folks would know she wasn't from around here, because Hithadhel was such a small, insular place when you got down to it, but sailors came and went constantly, and didn't always return on the same ship they went out on.

And Phoward should remember her, assuming that he was still in business and nobody had ever connected him with some of the things he'd done over a lifetime of covert criminal activity.

Man ran Arkez Machinery. Machine shop capable of handling anything from horse farrier up to starship repair, because this far from industrial planets, you gotta make do.

And they had horses on Astarte III, though nowhere close to the city. Farm country, where they were occasionally working beasts and frequently raised for shows by rich folks.

His shop backed onto the harbor, down and around some from the center of things. Exactly the spot you wanted to be in, if you needed to keep a low profile when quiet boats came and went at night, not always filling out the right excise and import/export forms in the process.

Not that she had any experience with that sort of thing.

Still, it was positively weird to be operating under orders this time, instead of dodging officers and offering vague, bull-shit excuses for things if she got caught. Somebody had been paying attention. And liked her enough to have her in with the Shipfitter herself for a brief chat. And no yelling, for once.

Day was late in the afternoon. That stretch when folks weren't all that sharp, looking forward to the end of their workday and maybe a drink. Or not yet awake for the nocturnal predators.

Adrian was mostly sliding along side streets. Not the alleys where things were a little messy. Not the main streets where folks were a little too sharp, a lot of the time.

Off to one side, as it were, emotionally as well as physically.

And, because she'd done this a time or two, Adrian went ahead and walked a double square inward around Phoward's place, looking for folks that were watching him or his clients. You never knew in this town. Or any of the others.

Nobody had stood out, so either they were good, or they were low profile. She didn't figure folks had missed Phoward, so likely he had his bribes up to date and hadn't crossed anybody important recently.

Still, she came in on the landside door, rather than dock-side, assuming someone in the harbor was watching smugglers. Door rang over her head. Old fashioned brass with a ringer, hanging on a spring such that it would require a lot of patience to get open silently.

And really hard to disarm by killing power to the alarm systems. In line with the Phoward she remembered.

Open space up front with some chairs and a table holding old magazines. Counter across the room, dividing, with all the important stuff in back, where you asked someone politely for it and they looked the part number up.

Counter. Phoward. Sleepy looking, grumpy looking old man resting his ass on a stool, watching her approach with wary eyes. Pale skin so much lighter than hers. *Wronlori* skin colors. Light brown hair gone gray gone silver gone white.

Eyes like a hawk.

"Hey, kid," he said, suddenly brightening up. "Heard that the Directorate was in town. Didn't realize it was your boat."

Adrian nodded and leaned a little weight on the counter. Phoward never called it *A'Zedi*. Always *The Directorate*. Similarly, *Wronlori* was always *The Technocracy*. Weird guy, but useful.

"Keeping a low profile," Adrian replied. "Me and the boat both."

"Oh?" he perked up.

"*Wronlori* been poking around in a couple of nearby sectors, so Survey sent us to wander around a bit and make sure they weren't building a base or anything around here," she said, repeating the lies Kimmel had given her to seed the local gossip mill.

Misdirections piled on innuendo piled on bullshit. Adrian's kind of thing.

Phoward's face got still and growly. She didn't know his story, but figured that he was another exile from the *Technocracy*. They had lots and lots of those, but that was Government-By-Asshole. After thirty-plus years, he likely wasn't any sort of deep-cover agent. If so, it was still a load of hokum to chew on.

"So what brings you to my shop?" he asked in a delicate voice.

"Got a new CO," she replied. "Oddball. Wants to do some things that aren't entirely in the regs, but keep it under the table if he can. Shipfitter sent me out to scout and see if we could find some parts for cheap, in order to build a few doohickeys that keep him entertained."

"Such as?" he leaned forward.

"Got a list," Adrian said, pulling it out of her pocket and sliding it across the counter.

Phoward pulled it below sight to read.

"Metal stock will be easy enough," he said after a moment. "In all those shapes and sizes. Wiring, too. What the hell does he need a Galloway Fabritronics Model Six Auxiliary Power Unit for?"

"Honestly?" Adrian asked, causing Phoward to look up sharply, then nod. "He wants the Hull Department to build him a boat. Sail on water kind. We can fake parts of it, but need power. Machinist designed the smallest thing she could, because we gotta disassemble it most of the time for storage. Claims the Six is the only way to do the job."

He looked at her askance, but Adrian had years of experience feeding people lines of complete bullshit. And this one was even mostly true, because they were apparently going to buy the stuff on her list, entirely as a cover.

Idly, Adrian wondered what sorts of trouble she might get up to, with a CO who wasn't a complete berk. And what other sorts of gear she might ask Phoward to find for her, if she was turning into an official under-the-table black marketeer instead of doing it as a side gig.

The possibilities made her want to cackle. She kept her face neutral and pleasant for now.

"How soon do you need this stuff?" he asked.

"Everything hinges on the Six," she replied carefully. "Until we can get a power unit, the rest is taking up space on the boat. Because we're doing this off the books, boss handed me a list and closed her eyes."

Phoward grinned at that. Lots of business went down that way. At least his business. But he did a little of everything, and had his hands in all sorts of stuff. Knew everybody. Hopefully, they liked him, because she didn't remember him having something like a Six in stock before, so he'd have to poke around.

Kimmel had warned her that folks might get a little twitchy about dealing stolen goods to an *A'Zedi* warship. Adrian figured that most of them would see it as a game and laugh themselves silly.

Without every realizing how deep these waters were running.

"Lemme make a few calls and see what I can find for you," Phoward said. "You check back here day after tomorrow. How long is the boat in harbor?"

"My understanding is at least a week," she told him. "Fresh from drydock, but CO wants everything taken apart and inspected by the crew to see what the yard birds messed up. Safest on dry ground."

Phoward laughed.

"We should be in good shape then," he said.

She nodded and sidled back out the door, covertly looking both directions before starting down the street at a meandering amble.

Down two blocks, she slipped into a teashop and lined up to order something warm. She wasn't surprised when Serge

Broom stepped into line two people behind her, nodding companionably when she looked back.

Man had been invisible, tracking her.

Well, tracking anyone tracking her, but him appearing meant that he thought her backtrail was clear enough, so Adrian relaxed some.

Nothing she was doing was illegal.

Yet.

But the day was young.

TWENTY-FIVE

Maddox had Armiger Freya Vilchis in his Map Room, listening to her latest reports from town. In Fleet Operations, the commanding officer frequently was the interface with local government. Transport Command let Captain Boru send his Stevedore, Kaitlin Lynch, to handle a lot of things.

Survey Corps did it way different, and he supposed that a lateral transfer that meant he'd never worked with a Diplomat before meant that it was all a little weird to think about.

Six divisions on a boat like this. Diplomacy got its own chain of command, because Survey was the tip of the spear. Out exploring and specifically talking to people. So he had a Diplomat. Freya Vilchis, the Armiger who was senior to Squire Rolland Waters as Radio Officer.

In person, she was pretty. Dark brown skin utterly without blemish. Black hair with just enough wave to offset the heavy thickness. She could have been a model if she'd been taller, but she was merely average height.

What had struck him the most was how she could turn *bubbly* on and off like a rocker switch.

Maddox got her gossip about how the local mayor had been so excited and interested at an *A'Zedi* warship come to port with needs and cash, but then Vilchis would drop back to clinical and it sound like the Purser going over his financial books.

"Does Mayor Thoran have any suspicions that we're hunting pirates in her harbor?" he asked when she wound down.

"None," Freya nodded. "She's a pretty face who got the job because she's really good at pressing the flesh and talking up the port and the planet to anybody that comes along. At one point, she asked if we were looking for a new forward homeport for *Doctor Kay*. I told her that it sounded intriguing and I'd make sure to ask my boss. You."

"Forward homeport?" Maddox asked, confused just a bit.

All the stuff he'd read and studied, and that was a new one for him. Lateral transfer from Line then Transport.

"Temporary base forward, like this," Freya nodded. "Outside *A'Zedi* lines on any map and *Unaffiliated*. Resupply and recreation, which Astarte is actually primarily geared towards. We sign a long-term contract and pay a monthly fee that reserves us a parking spot and generally gets us priority on consumables we need. Local merchants get to know the crew better because we'd likely have a standing reservation for a block of rooms at some hotel or something when we were in town. *A'Zedi* injects cash into the local economy. *Doctor Kay* doesn't have to return to base nearly as often. If Command decided that our mission was to start a formal scouting run coreward of Astarte, it would be perfect. Dunno if they'd actually go for it, sir."

Maddox considered that. Made perfect sense, so he must

have missed something and would need to dig up some books later to read.

"Don't brush her off on the topic," he decided. "But don't lead her on. I'll inquire home, but nobody has told me their longer term plans for us. Originally, this was a swing out to check buoys and make sure the ship and crew were in good shape for something longer. The derelict interrupted that, but I got the impression that I'm being sold as much rope as I want to buy."

"As long as they don't hang us with it, sir," she replied soberly. "It wouldn't be that bad of a deal, both ways. I know that nobody from Survey Corps has really subjected this sphere to a good update in a while. We only passed through last time, and that was two years ago. Usually, folks are operating on other frontiers. Or deeper rimward."

He nodded. Thought about it. Reached for the intercom. "Abbas."

"It's Nevin," he replied. "Could you join me and Vilchis in the Map Room briefly? Something has come up and your expertise is called for."

"Be right there," Abbas said. "Should I bring Rackham?"

"Probably a good idea," Maddox replied, then cut the line.

He grinned at Freya and she took the moment to fix herself some coffee, then shifted around next to him at the round table, freeing up space.

Astronomer Abbas and Astrogator Rackham appeared together. Sabeen Abbas was shorter and a bit bulky, but in fleet shape. Rackham was tall and skinny. Almost as smart as his boss, but he'd gone back for a MS in Astronautics, focused more on hardware than the theoretical physics side of things.

"Sir?" Abbas asked.

"Coffee and sit," Maddox gestured. "Informal questions

that came up and I don't have the answers. You two probably do."

He watched Rackham flinch. Abbas had gotten used to be asked as an expert, but the rest of the crew was still gunshy about that martinet. Nothing but time would fix it.

Maddox got them comfortable. Freya had turned off the bubbly and gone deadly serious. The other two picked that up quickly.

"Vilchis has relayed an inquiry from the locals about forward homeporting us out of Astarte III," he began, walking them through bits of the previous conversation to get them up to speed. "If we were to ask Corps to do something like that, where would *Doctor Kay* end up doing the most and best survey work?"

Then he leaned back and let those three talk. The conversation got technical in a hurry. Over his head in places, but he didn't need to be smarter than his crew. He needed to be smart enough to use their brains to accomplish things.

Finally, they wound down and started speaking in words he could follow.

"*Unaffiliated*, I will remind you," Freya interrupted as Rackham took a breath, deflating the man a bit.

"Right, so building out a series of watch buoys aimed at *Wronlori* probably won't fly with these folks?" Rackham asked.

"Probably not, no," Maddox agreed with Freya. "However, there's nothing to say we can't set general survey stations out. What could we learn if we dropped some generic, passive observatories in this vicinity and maybe out into that slice of space you two were talking about?"

Coreward from *Wronlori* by a ways. Put beyond Varfelis Station by a long sail. Spinward from Monsanch and those places he'd been with *Marrakesh*. Open darkness, he'd heard it called once.

"Generic, sir?" Rackham asked.

"We've got basic stuff already," Maddox gestured to the books and maps around him. "Anything we did here or there is going to at a minimum update those records, if not discover new things."

"What kind of things were you thinking of, sir?" Sabeen asked carefully.

"One of my last missions on *Marrakesh* found a lost colony of humans, well beyond *Traisan* space," Maddox replied. "Fallen from stellar tech to Iron Age over the last four centuries, but nobody really knows who they were before that. The sort of place that Survey Corps might drop this same sort of small outpost, while looking beyond them. Here, I would expect that you find more *Unaffiliated* colony worlds quietly doing their thing. Not lost to the stars like Sabahattin was, but folks who might appreciate an occasional visit from someone like us."

"Or not, sir," Rackham noted. "Pirates, and all that."

"I'm going to work on the presumption that most worlds would rather not have pirates around," Maddox replied, maybe a bit more sharply that absolutely necessary. "Smugglers are a different thing. That's a failure of tax laws, as much as anything. Pirates hurt people. Them, I want to smash, either us or by calling in someone heavy to do the job. Do you think that possibly basing this ship on this world as an anchor headed outward justifies the science and maybe law enforcement outcomes we might achieve?"

"Absolutely, sir," Sabeen replied. "As you said, lots of science we could do. I always assume that those worlds *Unaffiliated* themselves for a reason, but trade's trade, and letting merchants back home know who and what is out there builds stronger chains and maybe they turn into *Affiliated* worlds at some point."

Maddox nodded. He had the same view. Long term, because a lot of that would be measured in decades or generations, but Survey Corps had dedicated itself to doing that work.

After all, he'd studied *The Scattering*. At least what was known after old data systems degraded over time and historians put their own slants on things. Their own academic axes ground to fine edges.

And nobody knew where humans came from originally. Merely that they had seeded a lot of world over a mindbogglingly large volume of space, at some vastly distant period in the past.

"With only gear we have aboard, I want you to see what kind of observatory we might build," Maddox ordered them. "If nothing else, we can place it somewhere and file the coordinates for a future ship to visit. And I would appreciate a formal report on the astronomical possibilities of working outwards from Astarte III, so I can put that in my next report home. Questions? Dismissed."

He found himself quickly alone, but Maddox could already see the fire he'd lit under those three asses. It was good.

Hopefully, it would be enough.

TWENTY-SIX

Maddox actually managed to escape for longer than he'd expected, but a formal invitation had showed up, delivered to the bottom of the gangplank in person and embossed on a heavy cardstock by hand, so he wasn't going to insult the locals by finding an excuse to avoid it.

Thus, he found himself attending a private event at the Sabine Star. Hysmith and his crew were catering, all dressed in black.

Freya Vilchis had come with him, then been pulled away by Mayor Thoran as soon as they arrived. Maddox found himself being escorted by Stefana Davidovich, easier tonight because his cloak had been taken at the door.

Perry had sent Serge Broom along as an assistant, off to one side with the others, on call but out of the way. Maddox hadn't asked if the man was armed. Probably safer that way.

As she showed him around, Maddox got introduced to over a dozen local power players and their Plus Ones. Spouses, friends, whatever. It was obvious who were important and who were merely for ostentatious decoration.

The belle of the ball was the boss herself, Asya Orlova, who he had heard about but never met in the flesh.

The woman reminded him of a raven, curious, mysterious, and watching. She had deep-set indigo-blue eyes that didn't miss anything. Tonight, she had done her silky, chocolate-colored hair up in a bun, held with what looked like chopsticks. Orlova had an hourglass build, emphasized by a corset and skirt in a deep purple that contrasted nicely with her cream-colored skin. Tanned, but so much lighter than him that he almost took her for an albino for a moment.

Tall enough that she looked him in the eyes when he was introduced, but he couldn't tell how much of that was heels under her skirt.

He had to guess that she was an incredibly well-preserved fifty, though she could easily pass for two decades younger unless you looked close and knew what to look for.

"Knight Maddox Nevin, from the *A'Zedi* vessel *Blackford*," Davidovich introduced him.

"Mistress," Maddox nodded.

She shook his hand and somehow ended up on his arm instead of the smaller woman, but it had to have been planned because Davidovich swapped places with her boss like dancers. Then left them alone as Orlova began her own progression though the crowd. Eighteen people, plus half that many servers mingling, but the room was large enough to make it cozy without being crowded.

"Are you enjoying your time at Hithadhel?" she asked in a breathy voice that had him leaning towards her.

"So far," he replied neutrally, wondering what she was up to.

This woman, near as his people had been able to ascertain, owned the city. Possibly the planet, from the things she controlled and the amount of money she had access to, though someone else had the title of governor.

And Mayor Thoran was entertaining Vilchis across the way with some story that involved a lot of laughter, hand waving, and general merriment.

Orlova ran to quieter, deeper waters. You only had to look in her eyes to see that.

"How long will you remain on station?" Orlova asked as they greeted a local merchant and her husband, then moved on.

"I expect a few more days," Maddox replied. "This vessel was the last *A'Zedi* ship to call, and that's been a few years, so we've been busy updating all of our records and renewing old acquaintances. Plus making new friends. Mayor Thoran asked if we might make this a regular stop, but I haven't heard anything from my superiors, one way or the other."

She nodded, a bit dreamy, as if listening to a second conversation in an earpiece, but he couldn't tell.

"You would be quite welcome, Knight," she said in a way that suggested more than docking for occasional resupply.

Why she might be interested in him, Maddox wasn't sure, other than the uniform he wore. She was literally a generation older than him. He'd have liked to say his mother's age, but Mom still worked with her hands a lot, in a shipyard as a retired civilian consultant after thirty years. And didn't do *elegant* anywhere near what Orlova did. Practical. And a lot less curvy.

He figured that Asya Orlova could make women his own age look bad by comparison. Even in this room, with access to money and power. She was a diamond surrounded by lesser stones.

Maddox appreciated the way she was leading him around, as if showing him off. Even if it wasn't anything personal. He was just here as an official representative of one of the major powers in the galaxy.

At least as far as anyone knew.

After twenty minutes or so of chat, and a glass of really excellent red wine, they were seated around a hollow square open at the corners to let servers into the middle. Maddox wasn't surprised to find himself between Orlova and Davidovich, but he didn't think they had physical designs on his person.

Maybe.

Two incredibly beautiful women paying attention. At least his evening would be lovely, as he caught occasional jealous glances from the men and women around the room.

"What was that, sir?" Maddox asked as they ate. "I missed the first part."

Misho Pavlov. Local merchant. Power player, but mostly in off-world shipping rather than local. If Maddox had caught the references earlier, the man mostly traded into *Wronlori* from here, but the two nations were roughly equal distance away in a straight line, if culturally closer to *A'Zedi*.

"I asked if you were bringing more trade to the sector, Knight," Pavlov repeated.

Maddox hadn't formed a high opinion of the man before dinner. Crude jokes. Heavy, older man with a sweaty, bald head and a tendency to scowl a lot.

Orlova had whispered in his ear at one point that Pavlov was the kind of man who didn't understand the definition of the word *enough*.

"One might hope," Maddox temporized. "We're updating old records at present. Making new friends. Past that, I cannot say definitively."

He caught Orlov's subtle smile. Trade from *A'Zedi* probably threatened Pavlov, in ways that might be entirely in the man's head.

"Is *Blackford* a warship?" Pavlov pressed.

"A patrol corvette dedicated to survey work," Maddox deflected deftly. "Technically armed and capable of taking care of ourselves, but we're explorers more than anything."

Quietly, Maddox wondered if someone like Pavlov resented the pirates or perhaps had a quiet understanding with them. *Livingston*, after all, had come from an *A'Zedi* port, hauling *A'Zedi* machinery.

He added a little note in the ledger in his head to have someone look closer at Pavlov tomorrow. Might be interesting if he could dig deeper into the man's business.

Just in case.

Pavlov grumbled something under his breath and went back to his dinner with an aggression that looked like hostility. Maddox ignored it and turned the other way to find Orlova studying him.

She leaned in.

"Have they sent you to investigate us?" she asked quietly.

"Everything going on around here is mostly my own effort," he lied innocently.

Sins of omission, as it were, if Yadav needed him to play the cowboy role.

"And your next survey?" she leaned closer, as if depositing more of her perfume on his uniform. And seeing if that might include her?

"Playing it by ear," he said. "We don't really have formal orders at present as we work out a few things, so they've left me to my own devices."

An even less meaningful statement, designed to fill a conversation without adding any weight at all.

Except what someone else brought.

"But you might stay around a bit?" she pressed. "Return occasionally?"

"If we were welcome, yes," he told her, turning to smile and study her beauty from close enough to kiss if he leaned a little.

Utterly stunning.

And probably about as dangerous as a black widow spider, though he was only guessing there.

Not like he had a lot of experience with mature women. Or most women. And she looked to be a handful. And then some.

Maddox leaned back before he got in over his head and concentrated on his fish. Locally caught. Baked in a lemon cream with greens on the side. Rice and bread on the side.

Safer than the woman next to him.

He caught her grin out of the corner of his eye as she went back to her food as well.

Safe, for now.

He hoped.

TWENTY-SEVEN

Adrian had gotten a message through the grapevine to go see Phoward late in the day again.

The boss was in town at an event, and the ship was mostly reassembled and ready to fly whenever. Crew was a little grumbly that she got to go in and they didn't, but Kimmel had made it obvious that there were secrets they had to keep right now, which had gotten through some of the thick skulls on the lower deck.

She didn't have Serge watching today, but Sankar Bachchan was pretty good at what he did, to the point she only caught him out of the corner of her eye a few times, far enough back to watch watchers.

Side door, like before. Phoward, on his stool and looking like a sleepy merchant.

If you didn't know any better.

She let the bell announce her, then joined him.

"Got news," he offered abruptly. "Might even be good, but I never trust the second law of thermodynamics."

She grinned and nodded. Entropy and Conservation. Any change was likely leading to a breakdown, not a breakthrough.

But that sort of intellectual subtlety was why she liked Phoward.

"Found me a Six?" she asked, injecting just the right amount of excitement into her voice.

Not too much, because they were keeping a dipshit commander engaged and harmless. Not too little, because she had needs and wanted this done right.

"Sources place a whole set of them in a nearby warehouse," Phoward nodded. "Didn't arrive all that long before you, either, so the gods are apparently watching over your boss or something."

"They available over the counter or under?" Adrian asked.

That was really the important question. Over the counter and even the Purser could have put in a work order.

Under and you needed friends. Like now.

"Mostly under," Phoward nodded. "Import paperwork might be a little *irregular*."

They shared a chuckle. Probably non-existent and only faked well enough to get by, as long as nobody asked questions.

Adrian was familiar with boxes that fell off the back of trucks. It happened. Surprisingly frequently in her business, but she attributed that to luck and clean living.

Honest.

"If I can get something good enough to put in front of my officers," she countered. "And if it's cheaper than MSRP, I'm pretty sure they won't push too hard. Probably jump at wholesale price. Not like this is an *A'Zedi* world, after all. And we're just passing through on the way somewhere else."

Phoward nodded.

"Eight of them, new in box," he said simply, then quoted

her a price that was about half of what she'd pay, even FOB Astarte III.

And the freighter had carried twelve, so maybe a few had been kept back to replace old units? Or were already promised on to someone else. Under the table and at a discount, if you didn't ask.

"That's in budget," she said simply. "I figure you're getting a cut there?"

He nodded sagely.

"Then I'd be happy to get one," Adrian nodded back. "We operating through you, or is a third party going to contact me or the ship?"

"They wish to remain generally anonymous for now," Phoward informed her solemnly.

"Wise," Adrian grinned.

She reached into her pocket and pulled out a wad of bills that had been quietly whispering in her ear. Something about gambling halls and dancing girls, but she was on duty and needed to play this one straight. Boss boss hadn't been bad, but Deck Officer was on a bit of a tear lately.

Last thing she needed was to be confined to the hull for the next several stops.

Adrian counted out the cash, then watched it vanish below the counter and get counted again.

"Keep the change," she smiled. "Not my money, and still a bargain."

"Pleasure doing business with you, kid," Phoward nodded. "Lemme call them and a couple of other places to get your metal stock bundled up. I'll get it delivered here by tomorrow mid-day, then make arrangements to roll a flatbed out to the ship, probably late afternoon. Your sailors will have to unload it."

"They've gotten lazy, sitting in a nice port and sunbathing on the top hull," Adrian laughed. "Boss will love an opportunity to remind them that they're in the navy."

"Excellent," he said. "I'll send a note with an updated schedule tomorrow. Pleasure doing business with you."

She smiled and took her leave, getting out into the late afternoon gloom and walking lateral to throw off any potential tails wanting to follow her home.

Three blocks from Phoward's, she pulled out her comm.

TWENTY-EIGHT

Narayana digested Kimmel's report and gestured for her to sit. Map Room, though it was becoming more and more the place where all the various conspiracies were being planned and executed.

"And we trust that Stevens is on the level?" he asked his Shipfitter.

"We do," Joy replied. "I might have put the fear of several different gods into her along the way. She's always been a bit of a black marketeer, but generally in benign things, rather than crap injurious to good discipline."

"And Bachchan is in the field with her?" Narayana pressed.

Joy nodded.

"Serge Broom is with Nevin in town," she said. "Bachchan was next best for that sort of thing."

Narayana nodded and dialed a number.

"Security," Porter Zavaleta replied instantly.

"It's the Deck Officer, in the Map Room," Narayana replied. "Roust Pretty and tell him I need him and probably you, up here, immediately. Field mission as soon as you can be briefed."

"In motion, sir," and the line went dead.

"Field mission?" Joy asked. "Do you need me?"

"Answering questions," Narayana answered. "Pretty will run things."

Pretty and Zavaleta made noise jogging through corridors, then arriving.

"Sir?"

"Adrian Stevens just paid for our APU," Narayana said. "Bachchan is with her. The expectation is that her contact will call the warehouse where the thing is stored, then have it delivered to his facility, before it gets sent on to us about a day from now."

"With you so far, sir," Pretty nodded.

"Since we don't know who has it, your team will be in the field, surveilling the facility, then backtracking the vehicle making the delivery to Arkez Machinery, so we know who we are working with, in case they turn out to be the pirates we're after. I'll brief Nevin when he gets back, but he's our distraction right now, so his cover needs to be maintained. Questions?"

"Observation only?" Pretty asked.

"At present," Narayana nodded. "Remain armed, just in case, but that's a fallback. What do you need?"

"A couple of spare bodies that we can rotate through town to keep a low profile," Pretty said.

"That's on you, Marine," Narayana replied simply. "I need Kellogg and Horan for my bridge. You can have anybody else you need, but I need you in motion now."

"On it, sir," he said, then chivied Zavaleta out the hatch, bootsteps ringing on hull receding just as quickly.

"I feel like I've just opened a can of worms here," Joy observed quietly.

"You and me both, sailor," Narayana nodded.

TWENTY-NINE

Dinner had been lovely. Port and dessert, then a bit of coffee.

Somehow, Maddox wasn't entirely surprised when Orlova captured his elbow as others started to depart, drawing him to one side when he might have gathered up Broom and headed back to the ship.

Quickly, Maddox found himself alone with Asya Orlova, Serge Broom, and the folks cleaning up the mess.

Broom had an odd look on his face as he drew close.

"Status, sir?" Broom asked as he came to rest, pointedly not looking at the most beautiful woman in town, near as Maddox had been able to determine.

Maddox turned his head to look at her instead.

"Were you needing to return to your ship immediately, Maddox?" she asked with enormous eyes, all innocence that didn't fool him for a moment.

Still, all that and a surprising amount of brains, too. Felt like she'd won some sort of lottery from the gods, then parleyed that into everything. EVERYTHING.

And she was smiling at him.

He looked back at Broom and caught a whiff of something strange about the man, but Broom shook his head minutely.

"I don't believe so," Maddox offered, falling back into the role of cowboy he'd promised Yadav. "You'll get me back later with a ride or something?"

"A pleasure," she said, turning to Broom. "Off you go."

Broom nodded.

"I'll check in with Squire Perry, sir," he said specifically, then departed without a glance back.

Perry? Odd. Narayana should have the Deck. And if not him, one of the Squires.

Unless they were running some sort of operation and needed the Combat Team in charge. Petra Veillon would be commanding her guns in space, but Perry would be in charge on the ground.

Subtle message? Likely.

For a moment, Maddox was back on Monsanch, on the flip side where he'd had to rescue Captain Boru from kidnapping. Hopefully, nobody needed to do that here for him, but he'd burn that bridge when he got there.

Alone, save for all the staff, he turned back to Asya and smiled.

"I appear to be at loose ends for time," he offered with a smile.

Mostly to see if she was serious.

From the look in her eyes, quite serious.

Hopefully, he'd enjoy himself along the way.

THIRTY

Steve had gathered up his team, then grabbed a few warm bodies, like Lori Boyce. They were Lower Deck in the Crew Rec Space, with other sailors around the outside but keeping their mouths generally shut.

Armed troopers usually got everyone's attention, especially when he opened the armory and dragged some boxes down here and started passing out Type Three Personal Disruptors to folks rated for them.

"Sankar is in the field, watching our target," Steve began simply, studying everyone.

Helped that he was the tallest person in here. Lent him heft that didn't come from physical bulk.

"We will have three teams in place," Steve continued. "Harborside, streetside, frontside. At present, we do not know where our target vehicle is coming from, nor what it looks like, nor when our first target will take delivery. The box in question is a cube, 1.4 meters on a side, in an anvil case that should be painted dark green. It might be delivered by flatbed, and it might be in a panel van, but the latter is unlikely due to mass.

You will maintain a surveillance perimeter and track all vehicles arriving and departing from the facility. Since we do not have a ground vehicle capable of pursuit, I will remain here with Lead Expert Boyce, and we will undertake a training or test flight when we identify our target, using elevation to track. You have your assignments. Questions?"

He looked. Broom was in town, already hooked up with Sankar to start, just in case. The others would slip in, then rotate.

They didn't do this often, so Steve had already added it as a future training scenario, into which he would start offering certifications for other crew that underwent the training to his satisfaction.

Felt like Nevin was going to be bringing a bit more excitement and adventure in their lives again. Back to the old days, under Das, when he'd still been wet on his commission.

"Dismissed to operations," he said. "I want you filtering out every few minutes instead of as a mob rushing for the bar. Low profile. Go."

Then he was alone, with Boyce watching expectantly.

"You planning to take off directly from the launch bay?" she asked, which forced him to stop and think for a moment.

She could. Her flight bay had both top and side hatch, though the top was rarely used.

Except when sitting on the surface of a planet, like now.

"How noisy are you when you go?" he asked, trying to rate this for subtle, when there would be a shuttle riding thrusters in the middle of the night, potentially.

"If I'm not hauling cargo, we can get high pretty quickly," she replied. "I'll want to be clear of the landing field in a hurry, though, because ships coming in have right of way and tend to maneuver like pigs."

He nodded.

"You file a whole set of plans," Steve decided. "If anyone asks, you've just repaired *Packrat* and need to test various things, including instrument flight under darkness. Whatever bullshit you need to feed them. I'm guessing that Serge will need us if the truck comes by land, because anything in the harbor will be easy to track."

"Agreed," she said. "I'll grab a map of town and figure out where we can watch when we need, then plant my butt in the pilot's chair. You joining me there?"

He considered it.

"Yeah, as good a place to listen to radio traffic as any."

"Let's do this thing," she nodded, heading to the ladder.

He followed, wondering how it was all going to work out.

Or if this was a false alarm.

A good training simulation, if nothing else, but he had a feeling that it might turn out to be more.

Much more.

THIRTY-ONE

Maddox had retired to Asya's private quarters. Oddly, her personal space was above and slightly behind that big auditorium stage, with a huge, rooftop patio overlooking the city and part of the harbor, plus several hundred square meters of living quarters that almost felt insulting to call merely opulent.

Decadent, perhaps.

Like she'd handed someone a briefcase full of money and told them to spend it all. And she'd hired the right team, because the results were simply stunning. He felt like he was in a vid or something.

Of course, he'd come from a blue collar family, so this might be how you lived when you had so much money that you didn't know what to do with it.

His cloak was hung on a peg by the front hatch. She had drawn him into and through several open spaces that might all be one vast room, to an open kitchen, where he was on a stool watching her prepare adulterated hot cocoa on the other side.

As with everything else he'd seen her do, Asya moved with precise grace that was almost poetry in motion to watch. No wasted movements, though he still thought that she might be working a little too hard if her goal was his seduction.

Wasn't like he was about to turn down a beautiful woman. Hell, even Captain Boru had enjoyed himself with that one Knight off the repair depot, in spite of her being female.

So Maddox watched, and appreciated.

She seemed pleased at the attention.

Asya slid the mug across to him with a smile. He took it and sipped the utter perfection he had been expecting after everything else she'd done tonight.

Initially, he's wondered how a woman that amazing could be single, but now he was thinking that she simply had standards too impossible for most men to even conceive of, let alone match.

And Maddox wasn't sure where he stood.

"I feel like I haven't done anything to warrant this level of amazing," he offered, watching her drink and move like a ballerina.

She smiled. Warm and inviting.

"It is a small town, when you get right down to it, Maddox," she replied. "Stable, but gossipy. Everyone knows everyone's business."

"And I'm a stranger passing through?" he asked carefully, hinting at implications without actually touching.

"At least today," she purred back at him. "Perhaps your superiors will see fit to send *Blackford* around from time to time."

He was an outsider. That might be safer for her to indulge with him than any of the locals. Most of them that he had met at dinner were smart, but few had struck him for being *nice*.

Sharp, though, which you probably needed to stay in business around here.

"So how might I go about thanking you for the attention and everything you've done for me and my vessel?" he asked.

One thing that had stuck out in the briefing notes was how chauvinistic this region of space tended to be. *A'Zedi* was about as equal as you could get. *Wronlori*, for all their other faults, also kept things open for everyone regardless of gender.

Some places tended to consider women inferior.

Dumbasses, but nobody had asked him to fix the galaxy.

And he could only imagine what Asya Orlova might have accomplished had she been born on Horwin, the *A'Zedi* capital world. Probably be on the Directorate itself.

Her smile spoke volumes. Warm, but almost feral. Most men would probably be intimidated about now. He supposed that she knew that. It was in her eyes.

"We've had a chance to chat," she replied. "Dinner and such. Circulation. Showing you off, a bit, perhaps, before bringing you back here for a nightcap. How might you go about thanking me?"

He smiled.

"This is your world, Asya," he reminded her. "You are the most powerful person here. And a beautiful woman. And a smart one. And friendly. I think my job here is to place myself under your orders for a time and have you tell me what you need. What you want from me. How I can please you."

"Would you like that?" she asked coyly.

Maddox wondered at the verbal games, but supposed that they were all traps designed to catch someone playing games.

You never played games with a woman this sharp. You would lose. He'd fortunately watched a few other dumbshits make that mistake along the way, and learned.

"I would like to kiss you, if I'm allowed," he replied. "Perhaps other things, depending on your desires. What does a woman like you desire?"

She leaned across the counter and met him halfway. It wasn't much of a kiss, save that he could taste the hunger in the woman.

Lonely at the top? As a newly minted Commanding Officer, he understood that. Surrounded by a crew of highly competent professionals, he had to look outside for anything.

Same as Asya did.

She moved around the island now and stood directly in front of him, but put a hand on his chest to hold him in place when he went to stand, so he stayed put. Then put his arms around her when she leaned in for a second kiss.

More. Hungry need.

And he'd gotten lucky enough to be the guy she selected for a seduction.

Best not to fuck this up.

THIRTY-TWO

Narayana had gotten the full report relayed from Broom. Nevin delayed and possibly spending the night with the woman known as the *Sabine Star*.

He'd seen pictures of her. Hopefully, Maddox understood what quicksand looked like, rendered in flesh.

But then, Kumar hadn't always, either.

Still, Pretty had folks in town, both armed and merely wandering around with comms, watching.

He checked the clock and noted that he'd been on duty for twelve hours when Petra Veillon appeared in the hatch.

"You look like hell," she offered.

Narayana didn't doubt it.

"Why don't you go sit in the darkness for a few hours?" she continued. "I can keep watch over everything."

He considered it. And her. Medium height. Broad build. Black hair with a finger of gray she'd apparently had since she was eighteen. Smart woman. Pretty's boss, technically, but they did such different things that they functionally ran two departments under one name.

"How briefed are you?" Narayana asked automatically.

"Been talking to Joy and Camden," she nodded. "Lot of knives in the air right now, though I'm not entirely sure why we're going to all this effort."

He waved her fully into the room.

"Close the hatch," he ordered when she moved and sealed them in. "Because it's working."

"Working?"

"The crew bitching is down significantly," Narayana said. "They have jobs to do that require them to think on their feet. Some of them have forgotten. Others are like dogs on bones."

"I'm not sure how some of them tie their own boots, some days," she grinned. "But I agree that discipline has gotten better. Is that Nevin?"

"That's Nevin standing back and letting me get everyone back together," he replied. "He's letting me Deck Officer while he does command things. This is getting the crew moving. And it's working."

"And you look like hell," she returned to the top.

Narayana nodded.

"Too much coffee," he said. "Too much stress. Too many knives, as you said. So, yeah, I'm going to go to my cabin and turn the lights down. Won't sleep, but it might help. Pretty is running things from aft with Boyce, and they have my permission to launch *Packrat* as needed, and as many times as they need, depending. That's their hawk."

"Got it," Petra nodded. "I'll go check in with him and see what he needs. You go relax. I'd say take a shower or something, but I know you."

Narayana grinned at that. With most of the crew, he was something of a favorite uncle, at least until it came time for disciplinary actions, which he also ran.

At the same time, all the officers were nieces and nephews, and he got along with most of them. Finnegan Buccheri was who he was, and nothing would deflect that man.

Maybe he'd ask Nevin about replacing that one guy, while keeping the rest.

Right now, he needed some down time.

Because nobody knew when the flag would go up.

PART 3
TROUBLE

THIRTY-THREE

Serge figured he probably knew the town better than anyone right now, on account of having to sneak around so much when escorting folks. Or protecting them.

Tonight, he had an alley where he could surveil the warehouse he wanted. It was dark, with a few lights on around the outside.

Dawn was about an hour away, and Porter was deeper in the alley behind him, covering his ass against muggers. Of course, muggers would greatly regret things if they chose to jump Porter right now, but Serge didn't say that too loud.

He wasn't sure whether he preferred punching someone tonight, or sitting here quietly and minding his business as Porter beat the holy hell out of them.

At least the CO was getting lucky, because he'd have called to check in if he was getting home before breakfast.

Serge could always send Porter or someone to get some takeout. Not like this town ever slept.

In his pocket, his comm beeped quietly and vibrated hard.

"Three," he said, giving his checkpoint location.

"Five," came the reply. "Flatbed on Fourth Street with a box, headed your direction."

"Roger that," he said, turning to nod Porter to pay more attention.

"Five, this is Ops," Squire Perry said. "Move to backtrack line of sight on target."

Serge nodded. Move to a space where maybe he could see where they'd come from. The assumption had been coming down Fourth, since it was the biggest main street out of the warehouse district closer to the land port.

"Three, starting an approach," Serge announced. "Out."

He cut the line and slid the comm back into his pocket. Porter moved up next to him, then faded into a shadow as Serge emerged.

Pretty had assigned him Position Three, with specific orders, so Serge started walking like a man generally sober, just not in a hurry to get to where he was going. Head up and watching his perimeter, because Hithadhel could be like that at this time of morning, instead of him doing a reasonable job of staggering and bouncing off walls.

Warehouse sat there dumb and quiet, like a big rock. Serge was across the street and closing when he saw headlights at the corner of Fourth. Timing was the key here, so he modulated his walk, speeding up just a shade as that flatbed came into sight with a black cube strapped down on the back. They weren't really that big, but they were heavy. About half the volume was simply holding it in place for transport, so it didn't get damaged.

Vehicle pulled up to a closed garage door and honked, then turned in when the door opened a moment later, so the folks inside had been expecting them.

Serge kept walking, idly looking like a man drawn by the

sound, so he saw the writing on the door when it hit a pool of light, just before disappearing inside.

Up two more blocks, he slid into an alley and crossed back an extra block, one hand in his pocket with the disruptor in case he needed it, but nobody was about.

"Ops, this is Serge," he said into the comm when he was sure he was alone. "I have a positive ID on the truck. And the backtrack. Five, move several more blocks up and establish a new post. We should have about half an hour before they are unloaded and returning."

"Serge, copy that," Perry replied. "Who are we looking for?"

"Organization belonging to a guy the CO met at dinner," Serge said. "Last name Pavlov, so should be easy to find. I seem to remember a warehouse quad by that name on the maps."

"Stand by. Okay, confirmed. Five, I need you at Fourth and Chandler. There is a coffee shop that should have the line of sight I need. Go to ground and disappear. Serge, you walking that direction?"

"Affirmative, sir," Serge replied.

Time for a potty break, coffee, and maybe a pastry, depending on how quickly that truck got unloaded.

And if they came back this direction.

THIRTY-FOUR

Steve had a timer in his head, so he was just about to zero when Porter called.

"Ops, this is Three," the man said. "Confirmation. Target backtracking."

The comms were secured, though Nevin had mentioned some things his previous Radio Officer had been able to do. And how genius the woman was, so he didn't figure that there was anybody on this planet capable of listening in.

Still, best to use obscure language and code words.

That flatbed had left the warehouse and was headed back up Fourth right now. He turned to Boyce and nodded.

"Launch when ready," Steve said. "Need to be inland side of town, close to this starport. Our target is coming up Fourth."

"You buckled in?" she asked, but it wouldn't have mattered, as she brought her thrusters up and they were bouncing in the air like a surprised armadillo before he could reply.

Dawn was just about over the horizon. They'd see it if they got too high, but she kept it below two hundred meters. Down where skycars and airtaxis would fly, save that they were rare around here. Everyone rolled on wheels in this town.

Or on boats.

"Altitude stable," Boyce called. "Coming around on reciprocal course now."

Packrat's nose fell into line with Fourth below them. Not that far below them, either, as she was flying high enough to avoid buildings, but not much more than that.

One big truck, headed towards them, until it stopped at the place Serge had guessed, then turned left into an open quad.

"Do you want me to orbit this location?" Boyce asked.

"Negative," Steve replied. "Straight down this line to the water, then come about and head back up Sixth until we get back to the ship."

"Roger that."

"Serge, confirm?" he asked into the radio.

"Confirm, Ops," Serge replied. "I can even tell you which address, if you really needed."

Steve considered it. If this turned out to be one of the stolen APUs, then they probably knew where to find the others. At least some of them, according to Stevens.

Might be worth breaking in and stealing them all, except that *Doctor Kay* didn't have space without cramming them in somewhere and making crew life hell until they were carried back someplace else.

Still, it was tempting, being able to pay back those pirates. Or would be.

First things first, they had to make sure that they really were in the process of buying stolen goods.

It would look awful silly for the Knight to get back and discover that they'd simply negotiated one hell of a bargain on his new helicopter.

Steve doubted they'd be so lucky.

THIRTY-FIVE

Narayana watched Maddox come up the ramp to the back patio, behind the conning tower, with a smile on his face that spoke volumes about how his evening had gone.

"You look like hell," Maddox said simply when they were on a level.

"I'll tell you inside," Narayana nodded, stepping back into the tower where nobody could point a boom mic at them and pick up the conversation.

Once inside, Maddox got deadly serious like a light switch being flipped.

"Status?" he asked bluntly.

"We have completed the first part of our operation," Narayana nodded. "Paid for an item, watched it being delivered to the middleman, backtracked it to its probable source, and are waiting for delivery here to take possession ourselves and confirm origin."

"And you've been up all night supervising?" Maddox asked empathically.

Narayana nodded.

"Petra spelled me for a stretch in the middle, but that didn't help much," he replied. "Most of the crew that were out have gone off duty at this point, half here and half in town, where they are on five minute recall."

"How soon until the next stage?" Maddox asked.

"Stevens thinks late afternoon," Narayana shrugged. "Truck will roll up and we'll unload it."

"Anything else on your schedule, Deck Officer?"

"Negative, sir."

"Then you are hereby ordered to go off-duty until sometime after lunch," Maddox said simply. "At a minimum, at that. I can track down crew as needed on a boat this small. You'll be needed for the next pieces, so I want you sharp. Am I clear?"

"You are, sir," Narayana nodded. "How was your evening?"

"That was the most dangerous woman I have ever met," the man replied soberly. "If she has any flaws at all, I didn't stumble across them. Smart. Cunning. Beautiful. Rich. Powerful. And she is keenly aware of all of it. I figure I was the new guy in town, but nothing more, so I'm likely on call occasionally when she's feeling lonely and not much more. The evening appeared to go well, both the public dinner and the private nightcap *et al* afterwards. She has the potential to be a powerful ally if we play it right, and a terrible nemesis if we screw up. We done anything I need to worry about?"

"Followed the truck around," Narayana smiled ferally. "Tracked it. Serge says you met a guy named Pavlov last night at dinner?"

"Punk," Maddox nodded. "Fat, bald, sweaty, and mean. Highly successful. Shipping magnate if they had such things here, but small fry back home. Also dangerous. Different reasons, and second class to Asya Orlova."

Narayana nodded. Kumar hadn't always stopped to think about where he was sticking his dick, so Nevin had already surpassed him there. And seemed to be playing at an exceptionally high level.

This Captain Boru must be damned impressive. Or someone had gotten through to Nevin at the right moment.

"Pavlov was the shipper who had the APU we bought," Narayana said simply. "We backtracked to his warehouse and confirmed, but didn't do anything from there."

"Good," Maddox nodded. "Don't. We can't enforce our laws around here, and I'm not sure if he's a fence dealing in stolen goods, a pirate, or merely a guy who bought a cheap APU off the back of a truck. Since that's what we're doing, it will all become intelligence that gets transmitted home."

"Grinds me that he might get away with it," Narayana said, a little surprised at the vehemence in his own voice.

"Only for now, Yadav," Maddox said, suddenly ice cold. "At some point, if he's that deep into things, it *will* come around and bite him. Maybe we can convince fleet to send a Q-ship through that same corridor. Slow, fat freighter loaded up with turrets and troopers, just waiting to turn broadside to a pirate and blow them to utter hell."

"Would they do that?" Narayana asked, surprised.

"We're Survey Corps, Narayana," Maddox grinned ugly. "We find them. Fleet crushes them. I cannot imagine any legitimate system wants pirates around. And you've heard me talk about smugglers. Different ethics. But pirates need to be ended. If Pavlov has to be destroyed in the process, he probably should have made better choices in life, eh?"

Narayana nodded. Kumar had been like that, but had run hotter. A little less analytical in his mayhem and destruction.

Was that because Nevin had been in Transport Command and possibly a spy, before coming over here?

Narayana couldn't suppress the yawn.

"Now, you go sleep," Maddox reminded him. "That was an order. I'll sound the alert if I have to."

"Aye, sir," Narayana nodded.

Down the staircase and into the depths, where his bunk was calling.

They had a whole next Phase to handle tonight.

THIRTY-SIX

Maddox had noted how many smiles greeted him as he'd made a point to walk all the way forward to the Forward Sensor Array and Secondary Control Station, then fully aft to the Engine Room where a team looked up from behind welding goggles and sparks, then went back to whatever they were up to when he waved them off.

Back to the bridge, he found Perry waiting.

"Something you need, Squire?" Maddox asked, gesturing him into the Map Room so Kellogg could continue on with whatever training simulation she'd been running, without the conversation right behind her head.

"Checking in here, sir," Perry replied. "Figured you talked to Deck Officer, but he's been supervising from here."

"As I understand it, we're holding until Engineering or someone confirms that we've bought a stolen generator," Maddox replied. "After that, we still don't do anything to Pavlov's people or his facilities."

"No, sir?"

"No," Maddox said emphatically. "We're outsiders here.

Nobody hired us to enforce the law. What we are doing is attempting to trick someone in the pirate chain of theft into revealing themselves, so we can alert command and see what they want us do about it. Similarly, while we can try to find the pirates themselves by flying the line Abbas found, I will presume that they have a lot more ground fighters than we do, and might be equally well armed, ship-to-ship. Again, I'd rather drop a squadron of line frigates on them at that point and open them up like tin cans."

"What can we do, sir?" Perry asked.

Maddox studied the man. Tall, lean, and deadly. *Intent.*

"You've got people in town?" he asked, waiting for the man to nod.

"Serge Broom is my urban expert," Perry replied. "Got him scouting."

"Then maybe assume that our Mr. Pavlov is dealing with pirates," Maddox decided. "Have Broom start poking at people around Pavlov's edges and see if he can get more leads. And make sure that Stevens stays clear of that. I like her as a black marketeer, so we don't want to burn her with the locals."

"What kind of leads might work here, Knight?" Perry asked.

Maddox paused and considered some of the crazier shit he'd done while on *Marrakesh*. Mostly, him running the Gunnery Department, where he would have been Perry's immediate boss, but those had been things done for Intelligence Operations and not Line or Survey.

Still, it gave him an idea.

"Without mentioning names," Maddox began, eyeing his Squire sharply, "we captured a ship and copied out their entire sailing history going back several years. That included an unknown pirate base operating in close orbit of a brown dwarf kinda back in the brush, galactically speaking. Serge good enough to slid aboard one of Pavlov's freighters and plug in a datacore?"

"Probably," Perry replied. "But he wouldn't know the first thing about nav systems."

"Agreed, for now," Maddox said, thinking about some of the things he might task some of his crew with learning, if they were all going to be a big, happy family at some point.

Already, he could see them headed that way.

Maddox rose and opened the hatch.

"Kellogg," he called, drawing her head around.

"Sir?"

"Hit save and join me here," Maddox said, stepping back in and finding his chair.

Stenny Kellogg was tall and lean like Perry. Maybe ninety percent that man's size in all dimensions, so almost as tall as Maddox. Runner, he'd encountered her pounding out the kilometers on one of the treadmills below when he'd worked his weights.

"Sir?" she repeated as she came to nervous rest next to the Squire.

Dubious was the thing he saw in her eyes. Not that he was surprised.

"I need a thing built, sailor," he told her simply. "Doesn't have to be pretty, but has to work."

She nodded. Expert sailor, so enlisted with a few years in and enough gold stars next to her name to be his principal pilot in space.

"Squire Perry is going to recall Serge Broom," Maddox continued, drawing Squire Perry into things. "Broom is going to sneak aboard an enemy vessel, plug a portable datacore into somebody's system, make a copy of their sailing logs, then escape afterwards."

More nod. Not volunteering to go out where there might be hostile folks, but not quailing from it, either.

"And my job, sir?" she asked.

"Civilian freighter, Kellogg," Maddox said. "I have no idea what to expect or where he might find a slot to plug in. You think about how a bridge or secondary control space might work, how it might be organized, and what you'd tell Broom about how to find it. While you are doing that, I want you to head aft to wherever Squire Rackham is, and have him build you the unit that you will send with Broom."

"Me?" she squeaked.

"You, Expert Sailor Kellogg," Maddox smiled. "I know Rackham likes soldering, so he's likely to happily indulge. If he gives you any grief, send him to me or the Deck Officer. Am I clear?"

That last bit maybe came out a bit heavy, but couldn't be helped. *Marrakesh* had worked out because Captain Boru cared what you knew, not what your rank was. An enlisted sailor who knew their shit could offer suggestions to officers without fear of getting their heads ripped off, as long as they were smart suggestions.

Here, he'd put his principal sailor in a position to have an officer assist her, rather than the other way around. But Rackham was also a technical gearhead, and would probably love the challenge.

"Sir, yes, sir," she snapped to, head up, shoulders back, eyes on the horizon.

"Dismissed, Kellogg," he said.

She fled like he was chasing her with a whip.

Perry looked bemused.

"Broom going to need help getting in and out?" Maddox asked him.

"No idea, sir," Perry replied.

"Then you take charge of planning whatever Broom needs to do that part," Maddox said. "Off the books and don't get caught, but he's after a civilian operation, rather than military, so it ought to be a lot easier."

"Likely, yes, sir," Perry agreed. "And what are my boundaries?"

"Don't get caught," Maddox smiled. "If you do, Broom might get thrown to the wolves, at least publicly. Maybe thrown in jail for a few days, in which case I have to bail him out, or maybe we're declared *non grata* around here for a while and have to leave. I'll handle the political fallout if that happens. You see if you can get me another sailing vector that goes with the first one. I'd like to know where that pirate base is. Assuming that Pavlov is our guy, and I don't have a lot of doubts after meeting him last night. Questions?"

"None here, sir," Perry nodded. "You'll brief the Deck Officer?"

"I will," Maddox said. "Dismissed."

He watched the man walk out, and noted a new spring in Perry's step that was heartening.

Maybe, just maybe, they would come together as a crew, if he could point them at some outsider.

Some other outsider.

Maddox nodded and went to fix himself some coffee.

THIRTY-SEVEN

Serge couldn't help the way his face kinda screwed sideways.

"Seriously?" he asked Stenny when she was done.

"Freaked me right the fuck out, Serge," she nodded. "Even worse, Squire Rackham started cackling and might have gone all mad scientist on you, but I won't know until he's done, whatever he's doing.

Serge turned to Pretty.

"Yer all nuts, you know."

Pretty just laughed. It was an evil, ominous laugh. Like normal.

"Your second job is not getting arrested, Broom," Pretty smiled. "Think you can manage to get in and find what Kellogg needs?"

"Dead of night, late enough that folks will be drinking, either on the ship or in town, and thus not that sharp," Serge nodded. "Figure if I run a similar drunk on them, I can pretend to be utterly befuddled if anyone does cotton on to what I'm doing."

"Do you need assistance inside?" Pretty asked.

"Negative, sir," Serge decided. "Best if I'm alone, so I can spool out any line of bullshit I need to without worrying about a sidekick getting tripped up."

"I got a mean idea, Serge," Stenny offered, her mouth pulled a little sideways.

"Do tell?"

"What if you had a bottle with you?" she asked. "Filled with something guaranteed to knock someone out and mess with their short term memory. You take an antidote ahead of time, so you can drink with anyone who does catch you, if any do, then slip out later."

"Mickey Finn time?" Pretty asked.

She shrugged and Serge had to wonder if she'd ever done something like that. Or had it done to her. If it was the latter, they better hope he never found them alive. They wouldn't enjoy their short remaining time.

"Let me talk to the Doc," Pretty said. "Nordin probably won't go for it, unless an officer orders it as part of a mission. And even then, she'll probably ask Nevin for approval. But I like the idea and it covers your tracks if you do get caught."

Serge nodded.

"If I'm going back out tonight, I'm gonna need some down-time now," he said simply. "Been going for more than twenty-four hours and I'll start making mistakes after thirty-six."

"You take something and crash," Pretty ordered. "Kellogg will brief you when you wake up. Kellogg, save him some dinner if he sleeps through it."

"Aye, sir."

"Let's move," Pretty said.

Serge found himself alone, so he headed towards his cabin and hung the sign that someone was sleeping so the other nimrods would keep it quiet.

Exhaustion caught up with him about the time his head hit the pillow.

THIRTY-EIGHT

Maddox had a shit-eating grin on his face as he dropped down to the Lower Deck and moved through the crew rec space headed forward. He got nervous smiles back, but folks down here didn't spend as much time around him, so they were still uncertain.

Plus, he'd had an amazing night, on top of a day where his new crew was in the process of coming back together and turning into something that might make the bad guys really nervous.

Doc Nordin was in her med bay, doing inventory when he stuck his head in.

"Sir?" she asked, popping to her feet in surprise.

She was a small woman, but muscular, with shoulders and thighs. He'd heard her describe herself as a former horsegirl who enlisted to escape the farm and hadn't been able to afford veterinary medicine school, so she'd gone into human medicine instead. The *A'Zedi* navy didn't have many critters. Nor did the land forces that Maddox was familiar with.

E7. Senior Expert, because a boat this size didn't rate a

formally trained officer as doctor or nurse, regardless of everyone calling that position *Doc*.

Emergency Medical Intensiveness Care Technician. Good enough to run the machines that handled a lot of the formal diagnostics, plus maintain and distribute the usual medicines for hangovers and pulled muscles. Broken bones were rare, but could be splinted or cast as needed in the field, depending.

Maddox stepped into her realm and closed the hatch behind him. The crew didn't need to know what was going on.

"I have several operations in process, Doc," he said. "And need to go ahead and make this a formal order from the top anyway, because you'd have marched into my office and demanded approval if someone else had asked."

He had her attention now. Eyes narrowing and locked on.

"I am ordering Serge Broom to commit breaking and entering," Maddox said simply. "Someone suggested that he carry a flask of alcohol with him that had some sort of powerful sedative already dissolved in it, that he could share with others, himself having taken some sort of antidote ahead of time."

"Broom is slipping someone a Mickey?" she asked, surprised.

"On my orders, Nordin," he reminded her sternly. "Past that, I have no idea how he would do it, and need your expertise."

She blinked. Again, everyone saw him with eyes calibrated to Senoky. At least he was surprising them in good ways.

"Chloral hydrate?" she asked.

Maddox simply shrugged, palms in the air.

"Like I would know, Doc?" he asked.

"Right," she nodded. "Got something here, because occasionally folks need more than the hair of the dog in the morning. Serge can take it just before he leaves, and no amount of alcohol will affect him. I can add a few more things as blockers, assuming he eats a meal heavy on carbs, too. When?"

"You work with Stenny Kellogg and Squire Perry," Maddox told her. "They are running that part of the operation for me. Deck Officer Yadav will also know when he wakes up. I may or may not be in my Map Room, but am always on duty while aboard, so do not hesitate to bounce any serious questions to the top. Everything you are doing is specifically under my direct orders, sailor. Remember that if anyone gives you grief later."

"Sir, yes, sir," she nodded.

Maddox smiled and opened the hatch, slipping back out and smiling some more. Predator, surrounded by mice, but he didn't need to say that to them. They'd come around and turn into a plague of kittens at some point. Or wouldn't.

But he could feel the shape of the thing starting to come into being.

And placing Doc Nordin under orders meant that she could blame him for everything if it went wrong later, so they both had to trust each other. That was the basis of everything he needed here, anyway.

Them trusting him, so he could trust them.

And if it took a crime spree to manage it, well, them was the breaks.

THIRTY-NINE

Serge had his civilian, going-into-town clothes on tonight. Would have liked to have a few drinks, but Doc's shot had guaranteed that nothing he drank would matter. And probably come across pretty nasty from what she'd warned him about.

Still, he had some moonshine from the engineers. Raw stuff. Pure ethanol cut down enough that you wouldn't immediately catch fire drinking it, but nobody would taste the crap Doc had added.

He still didn't know how Kellogg had gotten to be an expert, and now was not the time to ask her. Later, when all this was done.

Still, he was in darker clothing. Stuff that would make him hard to spot when he was trying to blend in without actually hiding. Silver flask tucked into his hip pocket, opposite his ground cash. All set to go out and have fun.

Or something.

"Questions?" Kellogg finally asked as she finished, like she was running things, even with Pretty looming over her shoulder.

"Nope," he replied. "I assume folks floating around watching without getting involved?"

"I'm one of them," she said. "I'd have taken Boyce into town, but she has to be here in case we need *Packrat* on the fly. Vanya and Porter will be close, but watching from the shadows, in case someone is watching you. Pretty will be here with more folks. Go."

And he went, still a little surprised, but Stenny was good enough to fly the ship. And had explained the doohickey in his front pocket. Plug it into a datachip slot and odds were in his favor that the system would query it, at which point, per Squire Rackham's mad science, it would spin up some story of electronic bullshit that involved asking the ship to provide a data dump from the nav logs.

Things like that, per Kellogg, were hardly ever secured. Why would it matter?

Indeed, unless you were a smuggler, nobody cared where you'd been.

Until they did.

Outside air had gotten cold tonight. Like, clear stars and a cold front, so getting down close to freezing again. On the one hand, a lot of folks would probably stay in, so the streets would be a bit emptier than usual. Hopefully, his target freighter would be largely abandoned with folks in town instead of keeping a sharp watch.

Per Kellogg, and she'd looked it up somewhere Serge didn't understand, Pavlov had six ships in harbor at the moment. Well, two on the water, and four on land, not really all that far from *Doctor Kay*, since the big ships were all relegated to the western side of the reservation, with the small stuff on the east, more or less.

And he couldn't just walk over. Cameras would record

things, so the ship needed plausible deniability later if he fucked this up.

So, into town. Drink some, without any chance of actually enjoying himself, then gone again. All the bullshit would be on the backside.

Because this was a performance, he went down to the Sabine Star. The bar portion of the brothel was actually a step above middle, while the prices were still pretty cheap. Most of the profit was upstairs, after all. Hell, even the kitchen was pretty good, except that Hysmith's bistro down the corridor was some of the best food Serge could remember. And pretty damned cheap, but that was a favorable exchange rate.

Serge got himself in out of that damned wind and found a spot at the bar, over in the section where it was understood that you were here to drink and eat, rather than looking for companionship. It let him watch.

He'd have freaked out to see Kellogg wander in if he hadn't already been expecting her. In uniform, she ignored him, but sat intriguingly close to the divider, such that one pretty boy walked over and chatted briefly with her, all smiles and laughter.

Serge focused on his drinking, keeping from making a sour beer face when he did. The shit Doc had given him had also messed up his taste buds something fierce, but supposedly it was part of a treatment for people with addiction issues, using negative reinforcement.

Like, yucky negative.

But he was Pretty's urban expert. The guy who walked through a village or metropolis like a ghost. Adrian Stevens was the one who found you things. He was the guy who you missed while you were watching her.

Third drink, he figured that he'd established enough of a

cover story. And was tired of drinking battery acid. He slid backwards off his stool a little wobbly. Kellogg was watching, but didn't admit knowing him in civilian attire. A bouncer looked, but Serge smiled and nodded to the man that he was in good enough shape to get home.

Last thing they wanted was a drunk staggering off into an alley when the temperatures were likely getting close to freezing or falling into the harbor, so Serge stood up, shook himself all over once like he was fine, and strode firmly to the door, specifically turning left to go deeper into the complex rather than out into the cold night air.

He had some time to kill yet, anyway. Found a bookstore, but nothing appealed. Wandered over to the candy store and bought a kilo of stuff from several hoppers, mostly because he liked a good bit of it and could swap the rest with others later.

Fashionably middle of the night, he set out on his stalk. Bit of a walk. Uphill in the cold, but he'd planned for warm clothing. Nobody obviously following him, but Serge was making it a little obvious at the moment.

And trusting that Vanya had his ass covered. And Porter, but Vanya was meaner. And he still owed her money.

Back into town. Dark streets, mostly abandoned. Not a lot of private cars, so folks had battened down the hatches and said *fuck it* to the cold.

He avoided Fourth, taking Third instead. And then taking a wrong turn he had planned when he got into the starport reservation. Easy enough for most people to make that mistake. Presumably he was too drunk to pay attention, staggering slightly for effect on any witnesses tonight or cameras tomorrow.

Reasonably damned good job of acting, if he was being honest.

Light and dark intermittent, with poles only illuminating a radius, then inviting you to the next one. Serge accidentally vanished between one pair. Whoops.

He let the night envelope him and listened for footsteps or vehicles. Just enough wind to make that a pain in the ass, but he sat for five minutes and didn't see anybody.

Good.

He slipped back to his left and into a thing charitably called an alley, where two stacks of shipping containers had a two meter gap between them.

Out the far end, he saw his prey.

Rimward Sarychev, which was a stupid name for a ship, but nobody had asked him.

Big beast. Wider than *Doctor Kay*. Maybe longer, but hard to tell without putting them side by side. Longer than *Livingston* had been, so he was assuming four bays instead of three. Daylight observation from the conning tower had suggested four big hatches, but he hadn't seen them open, so they might be welded shut.

Not that he wanted to make that much noise tonight. Heavens forbid.

Astronomer had also suggested that the engines were cold. Like, long-term ground storage cold, rather than idling while prepping for flight, so Serge aimed his stalk to the ass end. Fifty/fifty that there was nobody on duty aft, with someone holding bridge watch and keeping an eye on various sensor readings from up there, instead of back where Serge might walk into them accidentally.

He was also specifically unarmed, because he was a drunk who had walked up to the wrong ship in the dead of night, rather than a burglar caught in the act.

Regardless of the bullshit he might spin.

Big bay door. Two personnel hatches next to it, so he went ahead and assumed that the closer one let into the cargo bay and the bigger one was either storage or engineering access.

He was drunk, so he picked the engineering hatch. Or something.

Wasn't locked. Why the hell would you lock something in the middle of a starport, when there were probably people aboard, sudden piracy notwithstanding. One finger on the button and it retracted into the bulkhead, lights coming on in the corridor that seemed to run all the way across, with hatches at the end and both sides.

Serge staggered inwards, moving on to trespassing. Stenny had brought in a couple of Forslund's people to talk about rear control stations on civilian ships, necessary if something happened forward and these folks were cut off and in charge.

He suddenly walked like a man on a mission, studying descriptions on doors until he found the one he wanted and crossed his toes.

It opened, and there was nobody here.

Whew.

Working quickly, he identified everything Stenny had told him to expect, pulling his data-thingee out and putting it into the slot, right where she'd expected it to be.

Thing beeped once, then a few lights came on.

Serge waited.

Just in case, he drew the only weapon he had, the flask, and opened it.

Shit inside smelled even worse than the bar had, but that was the stuff Doc had injected him with.

He waited.

Then the hatch opened.

All by itself.

Serge very carefully froze in place, halfway to a drink.

"What the hell is going on?" a man's voice rasped.

Must have been more awake on the bridge than Serge had planned.

He turned a bleary eye on the man in the hatchway, noting the long wrench in one hand.

"Hiya, Kowalski!" Serge called with a happy drunk tone. "Got home early. Think I'm drunk. This is not my cabin."

"Buddy, you're on the wrong ship entirely," the man snapped.

Serge peered at him owlishly.

"Is true?" he asked, taking another drink of floor cleaner and smiling in spite of the nastiness. He burped loudly and blew a heavy breath at the guy.

"Whoa," the man waved with his free hand. "How much have you had to drink?"

Serge shrugged.

"Lots, Kowalski," he said. "Want some? Down to my last liter."

Companionably, he held out the flask, wobbling some as he did to keep the man's eyes on him instead of the device stuck into a port on the station beside him.

The man studied him for a moment, then stepped into the room and tensed, wrench in hand.

Serge ignored him and started humming to himself, taking another drink.

"Gimme," the stranger said, free hand out.

Serge nodded.

"Enjoy, Kowalski," he said, holding it out at arm's length and not once making eye contact.

Not A Threat.

The man took it and sniffed. Prime paint thinner, if you

wanted a hard, fast drunk to put your ass on the deck in a hurry.

The man took a sip. Sputtered.

"Via, that's heavy."

Serge smiled with his entire body, nodding like his head was a little loose on his neck

"Yeah," he agreed. "Jaxon owed me, so he got me some of the good stuff from engineering, ya know?"

"Wrong ship, man," the stranger muttered, then took a heavier drink.

Serge kept nodding, ignoring the man since they were alone and that guy had a wrench.

Then the wrench slid out of nerveless hands and clattered on the deck, same as the flask did a moment later. Serge went ahead and emptied the booze on the man's shirt, like a bad, sloppy drunk.

Behind him, the machine beeped and Serge pulled the doohickey out. Stuff went into pockets and Serge stepped over his pal Kowalski.

Or whoever he was.

Corridor was clear, so Serge walked right down it to the opposite side from where he'd come in, beeped the hatch, and slipped into the night.

FORTY

Narayana was still smiling. Everything had generally gone off without a hitch. Kjell had confirmed the serial numbers on the APU matched the stolen inventory off the freighter. Kellogg— of all people—had run a significant part of the night's operation herself, which pleased him.

He'd known she had it in her, but didn't think she had realized it. Not until now.

He had joined Maddox in the Map Room, while Kellogg, Pretty, and Broom were working on the bridge. Coffee was a dire necessity that he hoped would go away in a few days.

Let things calm some. The ship was technically ready to fly now, having had a week where everyone could adjust every single thing that had come up.

Narayana simply had no idea what Maddox would do next. For once, he found that pleasing, because it meant that his new CO wasn't so entirely predictable as to be boring. Nor was he another one like Senoky or Kosere.

More like Kumar Das. It was good.

Kellogg appeared at the hatch. A bit hesitant, but Pretty

followed her in. Maddox watched and waited, so Narayana did as well.

She moved to the table and brought up the keyboard, typing a long string in, then zooming and adjusting a bit before she stood up and came to parade rest.

Maddox smiled at her.

"Whatchagot, sailor?" the CO asked breezily.

Kellogg flinched, and all that brittleness flowed out of her.

"Think I found them, sir," she said carefully.

"Show me," Maddox said, standing like a predator about to pounce.

Narayana did as well.

"We're here," Kellogg began, showing Astarte III as a gold star and adding other graphics as she went. "*Livingston* was struck here. The escape vector that other ship took runs this way. I found a second vector in Broom's new data that suggests a regular transit to here."

Narayana watched her bring lines and stars out, fading a lot of the rest into the background.

And Pavlov's ship did sail to a spot more or less on that vector from the freighter.

"Anybody live there, according to our records?" Maddox asked her.

She turned around, looking, but was boxed in, so Narayana found the binder she wanted and pulled it from the shelf, handing it to her.

Kellogg opened it and flipped pages for a bit, then shook her head.

"According to our logs, it doesn't even have a name, sir," she replied finally. "Merely an alphanumeric designation assigned by somebody a long time ago."

"How long?" Maddox asked her. "And how do you know that?"

Narayana watched her spin the book around and slide it over to him, pointing as Narayana leaned to see.

"We use a different numbering system, sir," she said simply. "This predates *A'Zedi* fleet standards."

"Does is date back to *Riffrost*, or are we looking at something older?" Maddox asked.

Narayana recognized the name. The *United and Free Worker's Cooperative of Riffrost*. It had been one of the political descendants of the *Naara Theocratic Coalition*, after that one broke up.

A *long* time ago.

He and Maddox had talked some about the mission to Sabahattin, and what they had found there.

Odd that some astrogational records might be that old, but entirely possible.

"I couldn't tell you, sir," Kellogg said cringingly.

"Idle curiosity, Kellogg," Maddox nodded. "Excellent work. Perry, tell Broom that for me, too. I'm highly impressed with what everyone has been able to pull off here."

"What's our next step, sir?" Kellogg asked.

"We have reached the end of our rope," Maddox smiled. "I have to contact command and brief them about everything before we make any move. Deck Officer, you had a thought?"

Narayana didn't think he'd made a sound, but maybe that tiny flinch had been enough.

And all eyes had turned his way.

"Abbas, sir," Narayana replied. "We've talked about building a few generic survey buoys and putting them in places, mostly to listen. How close could we put one to listen in on this new target and maybe see what they are up to?"

"That is a *damned* good question, Yadav," Maddox smiled at him, then turned to Kellogg. "I want you to work with Astronomer Abbas next, Kellogg. You've got the piloting expertise here. Have him and Rackham put their heads together and see what kind of an answer they can come up with."

"Me, sir?" And she was back to nervous.

"You, sailor," Maddox replied. "I'm impressed with what you've done so far. Let's see how many gold stars you can accumulate in your record today, okay?"

"Aye, sir," she said, then departed without an actual dismissal, but everyone smiled.

Then Maddox smiled at him.

"Deck Officer, I would greatly appreciate it if we could expand her training programs, such that Stenny Kellogg has the opportunity to commission at some point if she wants it," Maddox said, taking Narayana's breath away. "I think she'd make an excellent officer, and never got recognized early on. We need to see about fixing that now, before she decides to serve her hitch and walk away, okay?"

"I'll see to it, sir," Narayana said, still a bit shocked.

A field commission wasn't impossible, even in normal times, let alone during a war where every warm body was treasured. Hell, they'd been so desperate they've even let Kumar Das get him back into space.

And Stenny Kellogg would thrive under that pressure.

PART 4

HUNTING

FORTY-ONE

Maddox studied the device, but didn't recognize it, beyond looking like they had welded part of a communications relay to a hunk from a standard buoy, then covered the one end up. Kind of a like a gray-green mushroom a little taller than he was, and about as big around.

"And what does it do?" he asked the room, noting how excited Abbas, Rackham, and Kellogg were to show it to him and Yadav.

Downside of handing someone a blank piece of paper. Sometimes they fill it in.

With mad cackling, he'd been given to understand.

"Generic science, sir," Abbas offered with a straight face.

"I don't believe that for one minute, Astronomer," Maddox grinned.

Infectious grin. Caught all of them pretty quickly.

"Creator's truth, sir," Abbas nodded. "What we do with said science is an *entirely* different matter, however."

"Gotcha," Maddox acknowledged. "What will we learn?"

"Mostly, it is designed to specifically set quietly in a spot right at the edge of survey range from the system Kellogg identified," Rackham spoke up. "Call it six light-years, though we'll be at about five and a half, so we have vision past them to see things coming and going over beyond, in case we get lucky and spot vectors to other bases we can track down later."

"Excellent work," Maddox agreed. "How hard will it be to deploy? And will they see us doing it?"

"I've plotted a course that is on the *A'Zedi* side of the line connecting Astarte III with our supposed pirate base, sir," Kellogg spoke up. "They'd have to be paying a lot of attention, and have tuned their gear pretty recently to notice us drop out and work. I'm told that we need about thirty minutes outside of Ghost-space."

"Excellent," Maddox said. "In that case, you get it all ready to deploy while I take Kellogg forward and get us back into space."

He nodded and she fell in between him and Yadav, much more calm and confident than she'd been that first day when he'd met her. Growing into the role of principal pilot on this vessel, which he needed, because she would in turn infect everyone else in ways that Yadav had started, but couldn't finish. Not while he was Deck Officer.

Maddox needed this reaching down to the newest Able Sailor he had aboard, fresh out of training school and no longer a mere Landsman.

Waters was holding the bridge when they got there, face expectant.

"Sound recall, Radio," Maddox said formally. "Alert the ship that we will be launching as soon as we have everyone aboard and accounted for."

"Six people on ground leave today, sir," Waters nodded.

"Thirty minute alert status in their case, because we kind of expected a launch, with about twenty of that walking back to the ship."

"Give them sixty," Maddox said. "If we're gone for a bit, I'd hate to rush them."

"Understood, sir," Waters said.

"Deck Officer, taking command," Narayana announced in that formal tone.

"Ceding command," Waters nodded, then headed back to his Radio room to work.

Maddox went back to the Map Room. Out of everyone's way, now that they had a better understanding of one another, and it let Narayana get them launched and in motion. Like a good Deck Officer was supposed to do.

He closed the hatch and fixed himself some coffee as he listened to the ship make those odd noises it did on the ground, with weather, sunshine, and machines doing their thing.

He dialed a number from memory and waited for the land service to connect, not recognizing the man who appeared on the screen on the other end, though he was recognized.

"Knight Nevin?" he asked simply.

"Is she available for a quick chat?" he asked.

"Stand by, sir. I'll check."

The line went to a picture of Hithadhel Port taken from about three thousand meters, out over the water and late in the day. Really a lovely picture.

Asya appeared a moment later. Smiling and simply gorgeous.

"Good afternoon," she said.

"Hi," Maddox replied. "We're about to head off on a patrol, but I wanted to check in personally and say thank you for the hospitality. It has been a most amazing two weeks here, and I'm hoping that Corps includes Astarte III in future missions. Please convey to all your people the appreciation from all of mine. And our hopes to do it again as soon as we're allowed."

"It has been our pleasure, Maddox," she nodded. "*A'Zedi* is always welcome to call, and I've only heard good things about your crew."

"They were all threatened with mayhem if they got out of line," he chuckled. "Plus, I was using it as a carrot for the ones that had already impressed me. Next time, you might have a few troublemakers that I have to send an officer to get them out of jail or a drunk tank."

"Which would be more like most of the ships that pass through," she grinned. "Don't be a stranger."

"It would not be my choice," he said. "Thank you."

"Good luck, and until next time."

She cut the line and he felt a smile warm his whole being. The more he thought about it, the more forward basing out of Astarte sounded like an excellent idea. And not just for the cover identity of a Patrol Corvette out surveying and protecting.

Nobody but Yadav knew about his other job, and even Narayana only had bits and pieces he needed to understand. Kind of like how Chance Messier and Kaitlin Lynch had known enough about Boru and Taggart to help, without really going deeper.

Hopefully, he could bring Yadav more fully into the picture, but that would only happen after Maddox reported in the Permanent First Secretary and got her take. And her formal approval.

Still, bringing home news of a possible pirate base operating close to *A'Zedi* borders would probably be a big good star for the ship, especially as this had been originally intended as a simple training mission to break in the crew.

They'd gone well beyond that, but good crews did that.

Above, and beyond.

How far could they carry it?

FORTY-TWO

Narayana studied the readout on his screen before speaking.

"Kellogg, how soon until we drop out?" he asked.

Maddox had left the hatch to the Map Room open, so he could hear everything going on, but Narayana was running things. Deck Officer. Exactly how it should be.

It had been a while since *Doctor Kay* had actually worked like it should. Narayana was still getting used to sitting at the command station himself, instead of being elsewhere while Senoky tried to do absolutely everything, usually while screaming obscenities at the crew and belittling them at every turn.

"Two minutes, sir," she replied confidently.

Excellent.

Middle of nowhere. Recall had gone smoothly. Launch had been exactly on rails. Flight had been smooth and a little faster than normal, on account of Forslund and Camden Morgan retuning everything after a flight from drydock.

It was good.

Narayana rose and stepped to where he could look into the Map Room. Maddox was obviously paying attention, as he looked up from a tablet where he had been doing paperwork with an expectant eye.

Narayana shook his head, shared a grin with the man, and slid back into his station.

"Radio, what is our perimeter like?" he called.

For whatever reason, Freya Vilchis had spelled Waters this afternoon, so hearing her voice made him start just a bit.

"I have six vessels within scan range," she called. "Screen three. None are that close to us, nor headed in our direction at present."

Narayana took the moment to check. She had identified four of them tentatively as cargo vessels, based on vector and speed, with the other two merely designations for now.

Again, nobody close. Nothing in the immediate vicinity at all, which made sense, as they were about two light-years from the nearest star, and that one wasn't known to be habitable, let alone inhabited.

The probe they dropped would sit here quietly listening. Not a lot of real science, save that it happened to be close to a couple of trade corridors where ships sailing by could be logged. Maybe that one binary over there would be interesting, since it was a white dwarf/red giant combination, but those were almost a dime a dozen.

Nobody wanted to whisper the phrase *military intelligence*. At the same time, that's what this was, when you stripped away all the dross and innocence. And he had a pretty good idea that Maddox was setting this ship and crew up to do more of that in the future.

How much?

Survey Corps was supposed to be exploration, but he knew

that they did scouting for the fleet from time to time. And all this was all merely the extension of responding to the distress call from *Livingston*, a bloodhound on a scent.

Law enforcement was also on their list of duties, once they got away from Astarte III. Freedom of navigation and treaty commitments with various nations.

Part of the job.

"Sir, coming up on drop," Kellogg interrupted his musings before he squirreled in too far.

"As you bear, Kellogg," Narayana replied, reveling in the simple ability to do that.

Senoky would have insisted on every order being given by an officer, acknowledged, and only them implemented. By the book, which was how this crew had apparently driven the man insane.

Malicious compliance could be a bitch, when you pissed people off to the point that they insisted on orders for every single thing.

Today, Maddox was doing paperwork in the Map Room, and Narayana had just told Kellogg to handle it.

He couldn't help the smile.

"Drop in five seconds," she called. "Ship is in realspace, Deck Officer."

Narayana keyed the intercom.

"Flight bay, stand by to deploy your bird," he said simply.

"Standing by," Boyce replied, so she must be the one pushing buttons today.

Probably with her two officers lurking over her shoulders like chipmunks.

"Vessel has arrived," Kellogg. "Confirm destination within six-tenths of a light-second. Good enough, sir?"

"Good enough," Narayana answered.

Again, Senoky would have demanded that they turn around and spend a day or two sailing to the exact coordinates he had demanded, for no other reason than he was a punk drunk on power.

Not that Narayana had strong opinions.

"Flight bay, update your data and launch when ready," Narayana ordered.

The pause wasn't long. Probably a button push to transmit data to the probe, then confirm that it was ready.

The whole hull rattled as the VLS engaged. Vertical Launch System, because it was easier to send things straight up, especially when you were floating on water.

Then silence.

"Radio, new signal confirmed," Freya called. "Tracking true and stable."

"Flight bay, securing from launch," Boyce answered.

Narayana nodded. Just exactly how the book said you were supposed to do it, but today was really the first day he'd been expecting his people to act like professional sailors, instead of disgruntled mumps.

"All hands, we will confirm the launch and probe status for fifteen minutes," Narayana announced on a general band. "At that time, there will be further instructions."

Yes. The could do this.

"Radio, CONTACT!" Vilchis suddenly yelled. "Distress signal on line six. Pirate attack underway."

"How far, Freya?" Narayana answered.

"We're practically on top of them, Deck Officer," she said. "Screen five. Distance just under three light-years."

Narayana started to say something, but Maddox suddenly appeared right next to him, keying the shipwide.

"All hands to battle stations," he announced in a voice that had the implacability of an avalanche. "Engineering, stand by for a high-speed run. Gunnery, stand by to engage hostile vessels. Kellogg, plot a course and stand by to go to Ghostdrives."

FORTY-THREE

Maddox put a hand on Narayana's shoulder to keep him in the command station, as much as he wanted to swap with the man.

"This is your responsibility, sir," Narayana muttered, looking up at him.

"You sure?" Maddox asked.

All of this today had been for the crew's benefit. To get them used to the Deck Officer running things, instead of a meddling commander sticking his...beak in where he didn't need to.

"They'll do you proud, Knight," Narayana offered.

Maddox nodded back.

"Assuming command," he called. "Radio, do not, repeat **NOT**, acknowledge distress signal. Engineering?"

"We're ready for you, sir," Morgan replied from aft.

"Pilot, ETA to engagement range?" he asked, even as Narayana slid out of the station and started forward to where he could back Maddox up.

"How fast are we closing, sir?" Kellogg asked nervously.

"We hit Eight and change earlier," Maddox replied with a hard smile. "Repeat that now."

"Twenty minutes, give or take, sir," she said with a gulp. "We'll show up on their scans like a supernova when we light the Ghostdrives."

"Exactly my intentions, sailor," he told her. "I want to frighten them. Maybe they run. Maybe they don't. If they turn out to be too big for us to handle, we can probably outrun them to safety and call for somebody with enough guns to finish them off. Lock in your course and engage, then push the Ghostdrives, Kellogg."

"All ahead crazy, sir," she replied.

He smiled. She got it.

Only fire fighters and sailors rushed into danger.

Like now.

FORTY-FOUR

Narayana was headed forward when he encountered Petra Veillon in the corridor. The dorsal twin particle cannon turret was her station, with Horan aft on the bridge, mostly relaying orders and information between the two.

"He's really attacking into the dark?" she asked, pausing as he came even with her.

"He is," Narayana replied. "This is who I was expecting, honestly. Man was Gunnery Officer on *Marrakesh*, and that ship has seen more combat in the last two years than most line cruisers. He's good. He'd aggressive. And he sees himself as the protector here."

"Knight Errant?" she asked with a sneer.

"Why did you join the navy, Armiger?" he countered sharply.

She sobered quickly. Nodded. Turned to the ladder up, then looked back.

"We don't have the missiles to fight a pitched battle," she reminded him.

"All the more reason that he'll need you commanding the

guns here," Narayana reminded her back. "We've got discipline on our side. And surprise. Let's use it."

"See you in hell, Narayana," she laughed, climbing.

He continued forward to where his secondary station waited. Narayana could command the ship from up here if something happened to the bridge.

Creator help him if it came to that.

FORTY-FIVE

Maddox studied the plot, then rewound it a bit because he'd been pointedly staying out of the way of the crew doing mundane tasks.

Combat was never mundane. And as *Knight Commanding*, everything was eventually his responsibility, though he would have liked to know Narayana Yadav better before they got to this point.

One ship on the scan. Then a second suddenly appeared almost on top of them, chased for about thirty seconds, then both vanished, dropping out of Ghost-space.

Followed by a distress signal.

And, if they'd been paying any attention at all, a smart commander over yonder would do the math and realize that the ship rushing into danger this fast couldn't be that big. FTL speed was a function of mass, at the end of the day, and cruisers didn't hit Eight. Frigates might, if everything lined up exactly perfect.

That meant a corvette or smaller.

Would they run? A line corvette would have twice the guns and a whole rack of VLS missiles to engage them with.

Doctor Kay had a flight bay with probes, buoys, and other non-combatant gear.

They were still the *A'Zedi* navy, and answering a cry for help.

"Radio, status on distress signal?" he called.

"Got the one message, looped thrice before it cut suddenly, sir," Vilchis replied. "Nothing since."

Maddox nodded.

"Kellogg, time to intercept?" he asked, striving to keep his voice utterly calm.

Helped that he'd had Captain Boru seated behind him all those times, making it sound easy. He simply had to emulate the man who had probably done the most to turn Maddox into the guy he was today.

And survive.

"Four minutes, sir," she replied. "Nobody has gone to Ghost-space from that location. Does that mean they didn't see us coming?"

"Unlikely, but don't count on it, sailor," he replied. "They probably think that they can ambush anybody fast enough to race close like this, expecting some sort of small freighter. I want you to drop us long, and make sure you execute a bow-facing turn at the end, so the guns are centered forward when we drop."

"Close, pass, and circle one-eight-zero, aye, sir," she replied. "Programming now."

Good. He would have surprise, because they would be watching his approach vector, and at these speeds, they would have about one second to realize he was behind them.

Assuming they were looking.

"Horan, stand by to launch a Nine," Maddox continued.

Big missile. It would accelerate to terminal velocity while tracking on a target, then split into nine component pieces intended to impact. At those speeds, a big hunk of steel didn't need explosives added on, because the kinetic value alone was enough to go right through most ships.

Doctor Kay had a pair of Sixes and a pair of Nines loaded. That was it for total missile loadout. But nine pieces of steel closing at high speed should be enough to distract his pirates even more.

Any edge he could get.

Horan gulped like Kellogg had, but this ship hadn't been in a battle with this crew. Until now.

"Standing by, sir," Horan replied.

"Let Veillon know to center her turret forward," Maddox reminded him.

Petra had struck him as the kind of person that was already on top of things, but this was one of those measure-twice-cut-once moments.

"Aye, sir," Horan acknowledged.

"Radio, we're a scout," Maddox called. "Let's take advantage of that fact."

"Sir?" Vilchis replied, a bit uncertain.

"When we drop, I want you to point every scanner you have at them and see if you can blind them across every frequency you have," Maddox continued. "We've got the power to push. Let's use it."

"Aye, sir," she replied. "Calculating now."

Maddox settled and watched his screens as the distance closed.

Personally, he would have liked the pirates to suddenly start running like hell. That would have complicated his mission, but would have protected this freighter, and he was already in the process of doing something about piracy in this region, just by delivering that buoy.

Fleet would send someone to review the logs, and then maybe drop a couple tons of hurt on the place at some point.

No more pirates.

But that was tomorrow. Today, those folks had decided to sit and maybe play a little rough.

Let's do this.

Maddox focused on presenting an air of a man calmly waiting for the evening news to start. Letting his people execute, without yammering at them constantly.

Professionals.

"Coming up on drop, sir," Kellogg called.

"Gunnery, I want you to identify friend and foe as soon as we drop," Maddox called. "Lock on the enemy vessel and be ready to fire as soon as I give the command."

By the book, as this was the right time to follow the book.

"Standing by and locked in, sir," Horan replied with an unconscious nod.

He knew the book just as well.

Realspace.

"Radio, contact," Vilchis called. "Two bogeys. Scanning now."

"Gunnery, the small one is your target," Maddox said immediately. "Lock and fire both barrels immediately, then cool and go to rapid-fire."

Horan flinched, but pushed buttons. Veillon was already there, because the bow hummed with power as the first particle cannon fired, followed a moment later by the other.

Maddox watched the scanner wave reflect off both ships and start updating information.

One big whale, slow and wide, like that ship of Pavlov's that Broom had broken into. Next to it, a shark, half the size and streamlined in ways probably intended to intimidate someone seeing it bow-on with optics.

Kellogg had them broadside to both vessels, above their plane but bow-on where both the Twins and the defensive railgun pulsar could engage. Just about exactly perfect to ambush someone.

And the pirate had his turret pointed the wrong way. Maddox could actually see it starting to rotate on the scanner screen as Vilchis had basically aimed a giant searchlight at them.

"Engaging with rapid-fire," Horan announced.

Maddox nodded. Every hit now was to his advantage. Armor could only absorb so much, and he might have caught them off-guard, though there currently weren't any shuttles or EVA sailors in the space around the freighter. Better to take them down hard now.

"Continue firing," he said. "Our guns are fresh from a double refit, so push the cooling systems a little. Engineering, acknowledge."

"Already turned the pumps up to max, bridge," Forslund replied. "Dumping heat as hard as we can. You might need a sweater if this goes on long enough."

"Make a note to add that to emergency gear everyone carries," Maddox said, hearing a laugh from the folks aft.

Morale. It was all about morale. He had a loose crew, locking in and remembering who they were.

The pirate had taken one hit aft. Looked painful, but they weren't bleeding atmosphere. Not yet.

"Enemy vessel beginning acceleration on rotary thrusters," Kellogg called. "He's maneuvering to give us a smaller profile."

"Maintain current heading to provide a stable gun platform, Pilot," Maddox replied. "Prepare to maneuver counter to his spin when I give the command."

They were rotating on a flat plane. Let them, then he'd slide in behind and force them to overload their gyroscopes to stop and turn back. It could be done, if you had everything tuned and tested.

He doubted that any pirate maintained that level of professionalism.

"Standing by," Kellogg said a moment later.

"Gunnery, how are we doing?" Maddox asked.

"Two hits that matter, sir," Horan replied. "Starting to pound his bow and forward turret."

"Give him the Nine," Maddox ordered. "Fire it high so that no fragments threaten the freighter."

"Nine, firing high," Horan replied. "Stand by. Programming. Launch."

Doctor Kay vibrated down her whole length, then a new beacon appeared on his screens as the missile rotated, identified a flight corridor, and ignited.

One more thing for nervous pirates to worry about.

"Railgun teams, engage any launch from the pirate before you even identify it," Maddox called. "At least until you see them starting to evacuate the ship."

If they launched their own missile right now, two extra seconds might mean his people killed it before it lit.

Hell, if the two ships were any closer, the railgun teams might ask him if they could try for an extreme range shot on the pirate.

He'd seen weirder shit happen in battle.

"Gunnery, I think he just lost his turret controls," Veillon called.

Maddox flipped back to the right screen and whistled. Like

Doctor Kay, the ship had a twin turret forward, but one of the barrels was glowing in ways that didn't look good, and was pointed upwards at a forty-five degree angle sharp enough to be visible.

Then they were gone.

"Contact, enemy vessel has gone to Ghost-space," Vilchis called. "Orders, sir?"

"How is the freighter doing?" he countered.

"Minor damage aft, sir," she answered. "Comparable to what happened to *Livingston*."

Maddox nodded.

You could shoot someone in Ghost-space, if you got close enough, matched speed at point blank range, and got dead lucky. He'd managed it himself that one time at Varfelis Station.

"Confirm that they are not in an emergency state," Maddox ordered.

It would give the pirates an extra couple of minutes to run, but his first responsibility was here anyway.

"Stand by," Vilchis said.

"Kellogg, track 'em," he said quieter.

"Already in process, sir," she nodded. "Course locked in. They're fleeing at a little above Mark Four right now."

He nodded and smiled. She shared it.

They could run. They could not escape. Not at those speeds.

"Bridge, friendly vessel confirms status as functional," Vilchis said. "Damaged, but repairable with tools at hand."

"Let them know that we will be back in a bit," he ordered. "Kellogg, engage. Run them down."

And *Doctor Kay* took off like a hound after a hare.

Maddox dialed a line forward to where Veillon was commanding the turret, bringing her up on video instead of relying on audio alone.

"Sir?" she asked she she answered.

"Kellogg is going to overtake them," Maddox told her. "Then match speed and vector. I appreciate that we only have two barrels, but I want you to pound them from Ghost-space and try for a kill hit. I've done it on *Marrakesh*, but we had a hell of a lot more barrels then because we were hauling a Q-Module that day. Do your best, and understand that we can run them down in Ghost-space. Questions?"

"Negative, sir," she answered in a hard, quiet voice.

"Good luck," he nodded, cutting the line. "Kellogg?"

"Tracking locked, sir," she answered before he could continue. "Matching vector to provide a stable gunnery platform and maintain. What if they start maneuvering away from us?"

"Do the best you can," he said. "Radio!"

"Sir?" Vilchis replied.

"Transmit a message on fleet channels," he continued. "Encrypted. Ask if there are any warships capable of intercepting on this vector and assisting us in pirate hunting. Let me know if anyone replies in the affirmative, but I'm guessing we're on our own. Even a patrol frigate out on a shakedown cruise this afternoon ends things almost instantly."

"Acknowledged, sir," she said.

Maddox found that he'd stood up, so he sat again, watching and letting his people work.

His people?

Yes, his. They had made the transition. He could see that in heads and shoulders around him.

"Kellogg, time to overtake?"

"Ninety seconds, sir," she said. "Sliding in on him slowly to see if he suddenly turns."

"Stay on his ass, Kellogg."

Nothing to do at this point but watch. Everyone knew what to do. Book covered it, and they knew that as well as he did. Plus, he was letting them act instead of nit-picking everything.

The smiles around him spoke volumes.

"Gunnery, coming up on engagement range," Kellogg said.

"Understood," Horan replied. "Stand by."

Maddox watched on a targeting screen as Veillon dialed things in, then took her first shot.

Wide and high, but the reason you took ranging shots was to guess what Ghost-space was doing around here. Like a maritime ocean, Ghost-space had tides, eddies, and weirdness that made everything act strangely.

Second shot was closer.

"Target starting to maneuver," Kellogg hollered. "Trying to keep him bow-centered."

"Stay tight on him, Kellogg," Maddox muttered, not interrupting because she and Veillon had the most delicate dance in the galaxy going on.

Third shot went wide, but only because that pirate had turned suddenly in the instant before the shot went downrange.

"Gunnery," Veillon called. "Next salvo will split fire."

"As you bear, Guns," Maddox replied, ceding her the authority to do what she thought would work.

Engagements in Ghost-space were always tricky. Especially with as few guns as everyone had here. Hell, if the pirates repaired their turret controls while running, they might even try to shoot back, which was just nuts.

But he'd heard stories about similar things.

Forward, one barrel spoke. Miss, but then the second one scored a hit, tracking across the pirate's aft as his next turn wasn't fast enough to evade Kellogg.

"Drop-out!" she yelled. "Lost him."

"Turn and pounce," Maddox answered.

"In motion, sir," she said, hands flying across the controls like a concert pianist.

Even in Ghost-space, stars suddenly slid around like they were on ice, before settling back in.

"Coming in low and left side," she announced.

Maddox nodded. Any order he gave at this point would just slow things and confuse her, and Stenny Kellogg appeared to be in the zone.

He was happy to let that run.

"Guns, center to zero deflection," Kellogg ordered.

Ordered? Sure. She was flying *Doctor Kay* like an extension of her whole being right now.

Run with it.

And then they dropped into realspace. And there was a pirate right at the edge of cannon range.

"Accelerating," Kellogg said, then paused and looked over her shoulder, possibly aware that she'd been acting like the Deck Officer for the last two minutes.

Maddox grinned at her and nodded. She blushed, nodded, and turned back to her controls without a word.

He watched Veillon put a pair of bolts into the bow of the pirate. Metal exploded outward, white hot before cooling through the spectrum. And the pirate started a slow, corkscrewing spin under the jolt of that double hammerblow.

"Radio, anything from the pirate?" Maddox asked as a second salvo went unanswered, this time possibly aimed at the turret itself, because it detonated an enormous mushroom cloud that pushed the vessel into the start of a tumble.

And maybe just luck, but Maddox had long understood that it was better to be lucky than good.

You could be the best in the galaxy, but if the other guy got lucky...

"Negative, sir," Vilchis replied ominously. "Silent on all channels."

"Is he dead?" Maddox asked, quieter.

"Stand by," she said. "I'm not detecting engines or scanners."

"Gunnery, stand down and stand by," Maddox ordered. "If they fire anything, hammer them, but do not fire without provocation at this point. Acknowledge."

"Understood, bridge," Veillon answered. "Guns locked and holding. Railgun teams standing by."

"Radio, order them to surrender," Maddox continued. "Or be destroyed."

"No answer, sir," she said. "Been trying to raise anybody."

"Did we score a bridge hit and take out their command structure?" Maddox asked.

Silence greeted him.

"We might have, sir," she finally answered. "And the hit aft that knocked them out of Ghost-space might have gone through Engineering."

Well, hell.

Then it dawned on him that, for all its sleek lines, he was still looking at a civilian vessel. Made up to look tough, but not designed or constructed to warship standards.

It might be a ghost right now, if the damage at both ends had opened critical compartments to space.

Maddox opened the shipwide comm, because lots of people needed to get into motion right now, and he wasn't entirely sure where they would all be located.

"All qualified hands, stand by for EVA," Maddox said simply, figuring that they could figure out what they needed to do. "All security forces armed and aft. Flight bay, stand by to deploy *Packrat*, either for rescue operations or to kill spin on the pirate. Perry, acknowledge when ready to deploy."

Maddox leaned back and watched, but no signal emerged from the hulk. Whether they were playing possum right now or not, he had to send in troopers next to confirm.

Hopefully, help was coming.

"Radio, update fleet with coordinates," he said. "Anybody answering yet?"

"Negative on answer, sir," she replied. "Standing by."

Maddox nodded. Aetherial communications were ultra-fast FTL, but it still took time to reach. And decode. And answer.

Eventually, someone would, but maybe not fast enough to help here.

Doctor Kay was on her own.

She could handle it.

FORTY-SEVEN

Steve had already suited up. It took the rest seven minutes to join him, which was pretty good time, since many of them had secondary jobs and had had to take off aprons or put down tools and race to the armory.

Since Nevin had said everybody, he had Serge, Vayna, Porter, Sankar, and Trinity suited up with him, and Boyce ready to launch.

"We're going out first, Boyce," he told her. "Once we clear things, I'll decide if you launch."

"Roger that," she said.

Steve gestured everyone into the airlock and started a cycle.

Outside, *Doctor Kay* had maintained a reasonable distance, but apparently still had not detected any signals.

"Bridge, security team deployed and closing," he said into the command line.

"No change in target status," Armiger Vilchis replied.

Steve shrugged inside his boarding armor and triggered the nitrogen thrusters in his backpack.

Looked like a hulk. He could see some lights in a few portholes, but they looked like emergency stuff. Battery powered stuff.

Automatic. Nobody home.

He could also see places where *Doctor Kay* had stabbed them a few times, catching the bastards from behind and surprising the shit out of them.

It was also good for the gander, buddy.

"Spread out and watch for enemy troopers," Steve said automatically as they closed, weapons covering all approaches.

Nobody around. Tumble on all three axes of motion, but not really bad. Boyce could kill it if she wanted.

After he cleared her as safe.

"Zavaleta, on point," Steve ordered. "Let's try that airlock."

He lit it up with his helmet light to make sure.

Ass end of the ship was in better shape than the bow. Only one serious gash, but it went pretty deep. Not wide enough to slide bodies in unless he had to. Better the airlocks.

Porter slid ahead, then locked onto the hull with magnets in his boots, squatting down to tap the controls.

"Gravity's out, Pretty," Porter said.

"Figured," Steve replied. "Looks like most things are out. Bridge, are we reading any engine or generator power?"

"Minimal, Pretty," Vilchis replied. "Mostly battery power."

"Huh. Porter, make entry with Diseth, then clear and confirm for the rest of the team."

"Headed in," Porter said.

Trinity joined him a moment later as the hatch slid sideways, closing up like a mouth swallowing them after they got inside.

"Inner airlock cycling on auto," Porter said over the team line. "Got lights, but only about half, lending credence to battery power. Inner hatch opening. Nobody visible. Suit's picking up a lot of smoke. Making entry into the corridor, nobody visible. Battle damage appears as short circuits and local overloads. There have been fires, but no open flame. Suit says oxygen levels entirely depleted, so they put themselves out. Lethal air if you aren't suited."

"Roger that, Porter," Steve said. "Team making entry now. Hold your position."

Three other ducks followed him into the airlock, then into the corridor where Porter and Trinity were back-to-back keeping watch.

"Bridge, this is Perry," he said. "Confirm unhealthy status here. Headed aft to check Engineering first. Anything from your end?"

"Negative, Perry," the Knight said. "Ghost town."

Steve nodded and pointed Porter aft, walking on magnets because there was no gravity. Maybe a quarter of the lights were on, but they had suit lights for that reason. Harsh and white, they showed fog in the air that he assumed was smoke.

Engineering had taken a hit. Nasty one. That gash had entered the chamber somewhat intact.

Five dead people, if he was counting parts correctly. Only one whole. Everything charred, so it was probably instant.

About the only good way to die in a space battle, if your number had come up.

"Bridge, Engineering is a total loss at present. One hundred percent casualties, it appears. Headed forward."

"Exercise care," Nevin said. "Some folks might be trapped in side cabins, unable to get out. Confirm the bridge, then we'll put bodies aboard and see if anyone survived to be rescued."

"Rescued, sir?" Steve replied automatically.

"Better twenty years in a cell than two hours slowly suffocating to death in the darkness, sailor," the man replied.

Steve grunted. Not the answer he'd been expecting from Nevin.

Good one, though. Steve found himself smiling.

"Forward," he gestured Porter into motion.

FORTY-EIGHT

Steve entered the bridge once Porter and Vanya had managed to jury-rig repairs to get the hatch to open. And slid a prybar in when it hung halfway where the rails had torqued.

Looking up, he could see stars.

"Bridge, this is Perry," he said. "Command compartment is open to space."

"We confirm that, Pretty," Vilchis replied. "I can see your light reflecting off bulkheads. Any survivors?"

"Not even bodies," Steve replied. "Half the chamber has been destroyed by a through-and-through shot. Everything is cooked, fried, and mangled."

"Pretty," Porter interrupted, pointing at a bulkhead bulging inwards.

The hatch said forward turret, which didn't exist anymore, so he was reasonably confident that the hatch itself would be welded in place.

"You head up and over and look down, Zavaleta," he ordered. "Diseth, you go with him."

"Perry, this is Nevin," the Knight said. "Any likelihood of

secondary control systems in a different chamber that might be intact?"

"Maybe, sir," he replied. "Odds are that it would be aft somewhere. Gonna need Forslund's people to run some lines to be sure, assuming it wasn't cooked in the engine room itself."

He watched Porter and Trinity exit up, then walk out of sight.

"Boss, the whole bow looks like it's being held on by bailing wire and spit right now," Porter said a moment later. "I have blowouts and shattered portholes visible. Scorch where panels held when the overload killed them."

"Roger that," Steve replied. "You two walk aft outside and give me a visual inspection of any lit portholes you do see. Bridge, I think we're down to salvage operations at this point."

"Agreed, Squire," Nevin said. "I'll suit up some folks and have *Packrat* deliver them. You maintain command over the EVA operation and see if it's worth doing anything except clearing chambers for survivors."

"Affirmative, sir," Steve said. He turned to the others and gestured them back out into the corridor. "Time to start banging on hatches and see if anyone answers."

He doubted it. This place felt entirely dead.

FORTY-NINE

Maddox had swapped Specialist Sagan Dituri in for Kellogg for now, so he could pull her into the Map Room with Rackham.

"Sir?" she asked, off balance but not brittle. Merely confused.

"What you did with Pavlov's freighter," he began, waiting for both to nod. "Once Perry has cleared the wreckage, I need you two to find me the navigational datacore off that vessel. I'm hoping it survived, but we won't know until we get there. Forslund's people will be hands on, but I want them centered on that first and foremost. Once you retrieve that data, get clear and let them continue any inspection to see if the hull can be salvaged."

"Are we expecting any survivors?" Rackham asked.

Maddox grimaced.

"Pretty hasn't found any signs at present," he replied. "There might still be some, but that's his team's responsibility. I need to know where these people came from. Where did they homeport? Where did they fence loot? That's your job. Questions?"

Kellogg wanted to say something as he watched. To ask *Why me?* but held herself still.

"Dismissed."

Alone, Maddox reflected that knowing Nyssa Taggart had probably been one of the best things for him and Kellogg. He could recognize where Stenny Kellogg had slipped through various cracks, same as Nyssa had. Maybe had had supervisors who were sexists or morons. Something that kept them from realizing how smart she was.

And maybe it was just the assumed superiority of Academy-educated folks over enlisted. That happened more than was probably wise.

If he could get her to unlock her potential, his time in command of this boat wouldn't be a waste, regardless of *anything* else.

A shadow at the hatch resolved as Narayana.

"Status?" Maddox asked.

The Deck Officer was in charge again. Like he was supposed to be.

"Messages from Vhogga, sir," he replied, taking Maddox back to the fleet base where he'd first taken command of *Doctor Kay*. Felt like years ago, instead of only weeks. "Nobody is currently in a position to assist in the short term. Did the hulk rate a tow anywhere?"

He considered it. Technically, evidence, but nothing at all valuable past that.

"Transmit a negative, Narayana," he said. "I'm putting together an executive summary that will be ready in an hour or so, with logs and images, in case they change their mind, but I think we have everything in hand here."

"Agreed, sir," the man said, smiling and stepping out of sight.

For now, the hulk was a navigational hazard, but he supposed that someone might want to salvage it at some point. Once he knew where it came from, and who had owned it, he might even be willing to tell someone on at Hithadhel where to find it. It was the closest major port, roughly twelve light-years away.

And obviously, this region had a piracy problem that hadn't been getting as much attention as it should.

Right about now, it sure would be nice to have a line cruiser that could sail in a few places and crack heads together, but Maddox understood that the war with *Wronlori* would take precedence there. Probably what the pirates were counting on, in fact.

He just needed a way to turn the tables on them somehow.

Maddox went back to his report, trying to write things such that the Permanent First Secretary could decode it.

He had no doubts that she would be reading this.

FIFTY

Maddox didn't want to admit it, but being recalled to the big building that held Intelligence Operations actually made him feel better.

It could have been that massive estate in the middle of nowhere. He still didn't know who owned it, and pointedly didn't want to look that up. Ever.

He'd been here the once with Captain Boru and Nyssa Taggart. It hadn't changed. Empty space that could have held fifty on the empty wooden benches. Long counter separating three older civilians with scowls from Knight Nevin in *A'Zedi* purple. Day uniform, so no awards. Just rank and patch for *Blackford*.

The door behind the civilians opened and the Permanent First Secretary appeared. She seemed to be smiling. That was good.

"Nevin, could you join me, please?" she asked the otherwise empty room.

He rose and made his way through the halfdoor, following her into the depths of *A'Zedi* Intelligence. Or something.

Numbers on door. No names. Everything utterly bland.

Maddox wasn't fooled.

She led him to the office on the end, then pointed at the chair on this side.

He sat when she did.

"Close the door, Maddox," she said simply, waiting for him to do so. "I've spoken with Thaddeus, and gotten most of what I needed from your reports, but had a few questions. You left out a some details, Nevin."

"Those reports would be filed generally, ma'am," he said. "Secured, but I wasn't sure what level of security clearance they might be hidden behind. I know that *Marrakesh* is only officially Transport Command these days, so the Captain's activities are generally unknown."

"And you are correct that these might be more widely read than things Boru does for me," she nodded, turning as deadly serious as Asya had a few times. Both women reminded him of the other. "I'm interested in your followup on what your Astronomer deployed to watch for pirates, Nevin. Why did you not circle back and look closer?"

"We'd chased off and subsequently destroyed one pirate vessel, ma'am," Maddox replied. "One hundred percent casualties, but it appears that at least a handful were lost when the hull lost integrity in Ghost-space, and were irretrievable later. When I had my crew pull the nav datacores, they did not locate any references to the original target identified by the attack on *Livingston*. At that point, I presumed that I had an entirely independent, second pirate operation of some sort on my hands, operating in the same rough sphere of space. As my original orders had envisioned a simple shakedown cruise, and already been stretched extensively to include the investigations at Astarte III, I felt like I was pushing my luck as an officer and crew, as well as wandering a bit beyond any possible interpretation of my original orders from Survey Command. I know that the Marshall is paying attention here, so I wanted to convey to him that *Blackford* wasn't always going to color outside the lines. Plus, it had always been my expectation that attacking a pirate base was going to require squadron-level firepower. Or better, once we knew what to expect."

He leaned back until his shoulder blades touched the back of the chair, watching her eyes.

"And your so-called *scientific research station*?" she pressed, eyes at least smiling.

"When someone pulls those logs, they should be able to identity how many vessels called on that system," he nodded. "Possibly identify them, as even in Ghost-space they will have certain characteristics that can be tracked. More importantly, we'll have sailing vectors that can point to other, unknown bases or fences. I didn't figure I needed to rush right in with a Patrol Corvette, when it might be more than we can handle. Plus, this is an investigation into piracy across a wide region of space outside the Directorate's borders. And there are limits to my authority as a law enforcement officer."

At least she was still smiling.

"Keep this between you and I, but Thaddeus utterly lost his shit when he explained your outcomes over dinner," she explained. "Demanded to know if I'd brought in a ringer. I had to explain to him who Padraig Boru really was and more of what *Marrakesh* has accomplished, in order to mollify him."

"Ma'am?" Maddox asked, confused.

"He was hoping you didn't crash the ship on launching, Maddox," she laughed. "That you could tour a set of buoys, tapping them for updates, and make it back to base intact without your crew mutinying. That you uncovered not one but two piracy and smuggling operations just outside of our borders, saved one of the two ships involved, defeated and destroyed a pirate vessel, left him utterly speechless. And I'm not sure I've ever seen Thaddeus at a loss for words."

"Just trying to do my duty, ma'am," Maddox replied.

"And doing it exceptionally well, Nevin," she nodded. "The ship will be up for a citation. You will be receiving an award. And Thaddeus is far more amenable to letting me borrow you from time to time in the future."

"Ma'am," he nodded.

The crew would appreciate the recognition. They'd finally understood how thin the ice under their feet had gotten, but only after they'd gotten safely back to dry land.

He hoped.

"Which brings me to why it was necessary to call you in here directly, Maddox," she continued with a purr. "Tell me about Anastasiya Orlova. I understand that you got to know her rather personally while in port."

He couldn't help the blush. It redoubled when she grinned.

"She would probably be a member of the *A'Zedi Directorate* itself, if she lived on Horwin, ma'am," he began. Then continued when she pressed with questions.

By the time he was done, Maddox felt wrung out.

"You almost seem smitten, Nevin," she observed.

"It would be easy to be," he noted.

"But?"

"No offense, ma'am, but she might be the single most dangerous human I've ever met. You're a close second, and that's only because I don't know you personally well enough to move you up to first."

She nodded sagely.

"Good," the Permanent First Secretary said. "I was concerned that she might compromise you."

"I doubt it, but anything is possible," he replied. "Since I don't expect to spend that much time at Astarte III, we're probably safest."

"Oh, but that's where you're wrong, Maddox," she smiled. "I did see the suggestions in your reports about a permanent forward base for *Blackford* at Astarte III, and I agree that the benefits far outweigh the costs and the risks, as long as you understand what kind of woman Orlova might be."

"She literally has it all, ma'am," he acknowledged. "Money, looks, smarts, power. I don't know why she stayed on Astarte III, but she owns the place."

"That's why, Nevin," Gelashvili said. "She is a goddess there. Anywhere else, she might be merely another power player like her."

"Not sure there are many like her," Maddox muttered.

"And you are probably correct," she nodded. "But having you and *Blackford* that far forward lets Survey Corps do a thorough mapping and recalibration of that entire sector."

"Then you'll want to consider moving some firepower closer," Maddox offered. "A squadron of frigates that might be able to pounce on any pirate bases we find would be helpful. Against that second pirate, we had luck and aggression, but he could have just as easily been more than we could handle, and been chasing us instead."

"I will inquire with a few people, Maddox," she turned so deadly serious that it took his breath away. "Your next patrol is likely going to be a bit more focused, but I suspect that Thaddeus will listen to reason when I make a few suggestions. How is your crew shaping up?"

"Well, so far," Maddox said, still wondering if he was going to throw Finnegan Buccheri to the wolves, save that the man had hardly spoken in the last month, and then entirely business related.

Starkly professional, which honestly was all Maddox wanted out of the Ship's Purser anyway.

"No troublemakers?" she pressed with a smile.

"None beyond me, ma'am" he replied.

"Excellent," she nodded. "Let's keep it that way. Narayana Yadav really did get a bum deal from the navy, for things that were not his fault. His, however, was the place where blame was apportioned, and he has accepted it without any loss of professionalism on his part. He will likely never be promoted, but everything I have read about the man suggests extreme competence that should not be wasted."

"And I agree, for what it's worth," Maddox said. "He held them together, and brought them back when I needed them. *Blackford* has a solid crew because of him. I merely inherited it."

"Keep it that way, Knight," she said soberly. "I have plans for *Blackford*."

Maddox nodded.

So did he. And a wide open horizon that they might go exploring.

ABOUT THE AUTHOR

Blaze Ward writes science fiction in the Alexandria Station universe (Jessica Keller, The Science Officer, First Centurion Kosnett, etc.) as well as The Corsac Fox and several other science fiction universes. He also writes action-thriller (present day as well as historic). In addition, he's the editor and publisher of Boundary Shock Quarterly Magazine and Thrill Ride Magazine. You can find out more at his website www. blazeward.com, as well as Bluesky, Goodreads, and other places.

Blaze's works are available as ebooks, paper, and audio, and can be found at a variety of online vendors (Kobo, Amazon, and others) as well as the Knotted Road Press website directly. His newsletter comes out monthly and you can also follow his blog and his Patreon on his website. He really enjoys interacting with fans, and looks forward to any and all questions—even ones about his books!

Never miss a release!
If you'd like to be notified of new releases, sign up for my newsletter.

http://www.blazeward.com/newsletter/

Buy More!

Did you know that you can buy directly from the KRP website?

https://www.knottedroadpress.com/shop/

Connect with Blaze!

Web: www.blazeward.com
Boundary Shock Quarterly (BSQ):
https://www.boundaryshockquarterly.com/

ABOUT KNOTTED ROAD PRESS

Knotted Road Press publishes dynamic fiction set in exotic locations. Our authors cover a wide range of genres including science fiction, fantasy, mystery, literary, and poetry. We also have unique non-fiction voices in genres such as autobiography, business, cookbooks, and how-tos. We offer both DRM-free ebooks and print books for a global readership.

www.KnottedRoadPress.com

www.ingramcontent.com/pod-product-compliance
Lightning Source LLC
Chambersburg PA
CBHW070521100726

47907CB00004B/936